James Russell Lowell

Richard the Third and the Primrose Criticism

James Russell Lowell

Richard the Third and the Primrose Criticism

ISBN/EAN: 9783337419349

Printed in Europe, USA, Canada, Australia, Japan

Cover: Foto ©Andreas Hilbeck / pixelio.de

More available books at **www.hansebooks.com**

RICHARD THE THIRD

AND

THE PRIMROSE CRITICISM

"A primrose by the river's brim
A yellow primrose was to him,
And it was nothing more."

CHICAGO
A. C. McCLURG AND COMPANY
1887

I ASK you to listen to a few words : first, a few general remarks on criticism, and then an illustration of them from the play of ' Richard III.,' or rather from the absence of certain things in the play of ' Richard III.,' which, to my mind, seem to indicate that it is not Shakespeare's work.

I propose to say a few words on one of the plays usually attributed to him, — a play in respect of which I find myself in the position of poor Peter Bell, seeing little more than an ordinary primrose where I perhaps hoped to see a plant, a flower of light. I mean the play of ' Richard III.'

JAMES RUSSELL LOWELL,
Chicago, Feb. 22, 1887.

CONTENTS.

———◦◇◦———

●

PART I.

THE PRIMROSE CRITICISM.

" Your reasons are too shallow and too quick."

THE PRIMROSE CRITICISM.

"THE pale primroses,
That die unmarried ere they can behold
Bright Phœbus in his strength,"

may have contained virtues of beauty and
suggestion which escaped the peculiar eye
of Peter Bell. There may have been a language in them which to other eyes revealed
ideas of taste, design, wisdom, creation. To
Peter Bell and his Primrose Criticism many
another object of beauty in nature, art, and
literature has appeared to be but common-
place, though it bore the impress of high
origin, and carried in upon other minds exquisite sentiments and edifying speculations.
The historical tragedy of 'Richard III.' ex-
cites no admiration in the common-sense
mind of Peter Bell. He fails to discover its
poetic and dramatic merits, but, more par-

ticularly, seems to be oblivious to those masterly touches of energy and grandeur which
declare its author to be Shakespeare. Primrose Criticism assumes to be synonymous
with Common Sense, which is the only safe
guide in the study of any subject, whether
it be the Primrose or 'Richard the Third.'
It is to be regretted, however, that Peter Bell
has been so backward in coming forward with
his peculiar critical method; and that, as a
consequence, the world has been studying the
" thousand-souled " Shakespeare for three hundred years without the light of common-sense.
So uncommon was the sense of Pope, Dryden, rare Ben Jonson, and " starry-minded "
Milton, the poet-eulogists of our glorious bard,
that they accepted base counterfeits for the
genuine productions of his inspired pen !
So uncommon were the sense and scholarship of the distinguished commentators and
editors, — Rowe, Farmer, Theobald, Capell,
Hanmer, Steevens, Johnson, Malone, Chalmers, Douce, Dyce, and Knight, — that they
were unable, with a life-long study, to distin-
guish between the genuine and the spurious
plays of Shakespeare ! With their master-
ful knowledge of Elizabethan literature, and
their familiar acquaintance with the English

dramatists, they do not seem to have had the slightest suspicion that 'Richard III.' was not written in the style of Shakespeare, or that it was unworthy of him and must have been the production of an inferior genius.

Alas, that Peter Bell should have been so tardy in making his appearance ! But Primrose Criticism had to await the coming of Peter Bell, and Peter Bell the advent of Wordsworth. It is certainly only a coincidence ; but Peter Bell's criticism of the Primrose was almost identical with Wordsworth's estimate of Shakespeare. The author of 'Peter Bell' should not blame poor Peter for a dulness of vision of which he is himself guilty. On the authority of Mr. Buckle, Wordsworth once told Charles Lamb that Shakespeare was not so great as he was popularly estimated to be, and thought that he could, if he had a mind, write as well as Shakespeare. " But then, you see,"said Lamb, " he had not the *mind.*" Wordsworth looked upon Shakespeare through the very spectacles of Peter Bell, and

The primrose by the *Avon's* brim
A yellow primrose was to him,
And it was nothing more.

But to all eyes that wear not Peter Bell's spectacles the world never grew, before nor since, such another primrose.

" Beware (delighted Poets !) when you sing
   To welcome Nature in the early Spring:
      Your num'rous Feet not tread
   The Banks of Avon; for each Flowre
   (As it nere knew a Sunne or Showre)
      Hangs there, the pensive head.

" Each Tree, whose thick, and spreading growth hath
      made
   Rather a Night beneath the Boughs than shade,
      (Unwilling now to grow.)
   Lookes like a Plume a Captaine weares,
   Whose rifled Falls are steept i' th teares
      Which from his last rage flow.

" The pitious River wept it selfe away
   Long since (Alas !) to such a swift decay ;
      That reach the Map, and looke
   If you a River there can spie ;
   And for a River your mock'd Eye,
      Will find a shallow Brooke."

Valuable as common-sense may be, possibly the sense of man should not grow too common, if it would appreciate the most uncommon sense that ever yet was writ. Let it be admitted, however, that the unadulterated Primrose Criticism fully appreciates Shakespeare's genius, and even places him far above

the ignoble possibility of errors and vulgar
faults ; yet it attempts to stab to the heart
the most celebrated offspring of the poet's
genius, and then to deny its Shakespearian
legitimacy.

It is to be supposed that a shoemaker is
the best judge of a shoe, an artist of a picture, and a poet of verse. But while the cob-
bler's judgment as to the quality of the shoe
must be accepted, the soundness of his judgment as to the age and the maker of it may
be questioned. The poet may pass judgment
on the poetical merits of an ' Iliad,' ' The Faerie
Queene,' or a ' Richard III.,' but his poetical
genius and instinct alone are not sufficient
foundation for a judgment that must rest on
historical data, on antiquarian knowledge, on
records, facts, and logic. Let the poet declare on his judgment that ' Richard III.' is an
inferior production,—that it by merit holds no
high rank among dramas. Then let the critic
have the courage of a Voltaire or a Wordsworth and attack Shakespeare himself,—
point out his faults, expose his blunders, and
show wherein his genius has been overrated.
Here is critical heroism and enterprise. When
Peter Bell turned his unique optics upon the
primrose, and stared in upon its delicate

beauty, he did not have the temerity to argue
that as the primrose is nothing but a primrose, therefore the Almighty needs to be relieved of the responsibility of having created
it. But Peter Bell grows brave as he scruti-
nizes the dramatic flower known as ' Richard
III.' To his superb common-sense it is but
a rank and unsightly weed of low and vulgar
origin. " But, ' in the name of all the gods
at once,' charge me not," says Peter, " with
the unpardonable offence of imputing any
fault or slightest imperfection to Shakespeare's
infallible judgment and genius, because 'Richard III.,' you know, must not be attributed
to his divine, unerring pen." Sublime critical courage ! Marvellous veneration for
Shakespeare !

The Primrose Criticism lays down the new
canon that whatever a genius may do that is
unworthy of him shall not be attributed to
him, but shall be branded as a literary found-
ling. Happy the artist, general, statesman,
historian, preacher, or poet who may be thus
easily relieved of responsibility for his faults
and weaknesses ! But is this Common-sense
Criticism ? It is undoubtedly Primrose-sense,
and Peter-Bell-sense put to criticism ; but, in
the name of scientific and literary integrity,

let it be hoped that it will long remain very Uncommon-sense.

The arguments employed by the Primrose Criticism in its attempt to rob Shakespeare of 'Richard III.' are not sound. One argument stands in this shape : Shakespeare never wrote deliberate nonsense, nor knowingly indulged in defective metre. 'Richard III.' contains deliberate nonsense and premeditated defective metre. Ergo : Shakespeare never wrote the historical tragedy of 'Richard III.' With all due and unfeigned respect for him who advanced this argument, it cannot be accepted as sound and reliable. It suggests itself to a careful student of the Primrose method, that it would take very uncommon sense at this time to discover whether Shakespeare's nonsense was deliberate or not, and whether he indulged in defective metre knowingly or unknowingly. The discussion of questions of this character is as futile as it is unimportant. But if Primrose Criticism affirms that Shakespeare never wrote nonsense nor indulged in defective metre as a fact, there shall be a square issue, which may be settled without resort to any transcendental speculations. Shakespeare did write nonsense, and he indulged very frequently in defective metre. Peter Bell must be developing a supernatural power of vision in these latter days that he is able to discover in every production of Shakespeare absolute perfection of poetical form, infallibility of dramatic plan, unadulterated wisdom, and impeccable fancy. Surely this is finding " infinite deeps and marvellous revelations in a primrose."

There is not a play, among all that are attributed to Shakespeare, which can be said to be absolutely free from nonsense. Nor is there a single play that is absolutely free from defective metre. These are the very faults which our poet's detractors have most successfully proven against him, and which his admirers have most unhesitatingly admitted. Rare Ben Jonson was almost prophetic in his honest criticism ; writing, it would seem, with his eye on the Primrose critic of this far-off time. " I remember," says he, " the Players have often mentioned it as an honor to Shakespeare, that in his writing (whatsoever he penn'd) hee never blotted out line. My answer hath beene, would he had blotted a thousand. Which they thought a malevolent speech. I had not told posterity this, but for their ignorance, who choose that circumstance to commend their friend by, wherein

he most faulted." Editors and commentators
have been severely and justly criticised themselves for attempting to correct Shakespeare's
nonsense and defective metre. , The perfection of nonsense has been employed to
explain away the nonsense of Shakespeare;
syllables have been added to or subtracted
from his lines, and absolute prose changed
into verse to mend the poet's limping metre.
But the best editions of Shakespeare's works
at the present time contain, in almost if not
quite every play, instances of nonsense and
of defective metre which have fortunately
been rescued from the literary botchery of
over-nice emendators whose delicate tastes
and sensitive ears could not permit Shakespeare's art to remain in its original and now
valuable imperfection. It is the aim of the
highest Shakespearian scholarship and editor-
ship to permit this age and all the future to
know what this singer really sang, and to let

> "sweetest Shakespeare, Fancy's child,
> Warble his native wood-notes wild."

The metrical dissonance of an Alexandrine
or a blank prose line introduced into the harmony of heroic verse has often thrown such
critics as Steevens, Seymour, and Collier into

the very anguish of hypercriticism and into those emendatory spasms that have resulted in the infliction of wounds of metrical corrections upon the original text of Shakespeare's plays, which the best and wisest scholarship of to-day would heal and obliterate.

Primrose Criticism affirms that the original text of Shakespeare's plays could not have contained a faulty verse, nor a passage of obscure sense, nor a low, unchaste fancy. The conclusion is, that every such defect must be an interpolation, which originated with actors, short-hand reporters, and brainless critics of the Anti-Primrose school. This is certainly a *petitio principii*, if we are to ignore all the historical and scientific data on which an argument for the genuineness of the text should be based.

The scholarly judgment of Richard Grant White had not been bewitched by the Primrose method when he wrote: "Not what Shakespeare might, could, would, or should have written, but what, according to the best evidence, did he write, is the only admissible or defensible object of the labors of his editors and verbal critics." This is true common-sense applied to the study of Shakespeare; and no critic need fear that he will be "laying

himself open to the reproach of applying common sense to the study of Shakespeare," who
tramples upon this canon. It may require
an uncommon sense to determine what Shakespeare might, could, would, or should have
written, — and this the Primrose Criticism, in
consistency, should never attempt, — but to
determine what Shakespeare did write may
require simply that ordinary common-sense
which is to be distinguished from extraordinary Primrose common-sense.

The external evidences of the Shakespearian
authorship of 'Richard III.' are many and
indisputable.

In the Books of the Stationers' Company,
London, the play is attributed to Shakespeare.
Four editions of the quarto were issued during
the author's lifetime. The first edition was
published in 1597, according to the Stationers'
Registers. This first edition did not bear the
name of its author. It was published anony-
mously. All the subsequent editions, 1598,
1602, 1605, 1612, 1621, 1622, 1629, and
1634, bore the name of William Shakespeare.
When Shakespeare's complete plays were first
published, in 1623, 'Richard III.' was in-
cluded. Nor has that play ever been excluded
from the undisputed works of Shakespeare.

This is at least *prima facie* evidence of the
Shakespearian authorship of the play. If it
be argued that some doubt is justified by the
absence of Shakespeare's name from the title-
page of the first quarto edition, the reply will
be, that on the same ground doubt should be
cast on the Shakespearian authorship of ' Richard II.,' 'Romeo and Juliet,' ' Henry IV.,'
and ' Henry V.,' which even Primrose Criticism may not be prepared to do. At least
three editions of 'Richard III.' were published
during the lifetime of the author, bearing his
name, nor was any question then raised as to
the genuineness of the play. After the author's
death, as has been stated, this tragedy took its
place in all the folio editions of Shakespeare's
works, and has not in a single instance been
denied its rightful place in subsequent editions.

It is not altogether unimportant as an argument, that this play has passed without chal-
lenge the scholarly and critical scrutiny of
Rowe, Pope, Theobald, Hanmer, Warburton,
Johnson, Capell, Steevens, Reed, Malone,
Chalmers, Harness, Singer, Knight, Collier,
Halliwell-Phillipps, Hudson, Dyce, White,
and Clarke, — a score of editors and critics
whose several and united scholarship is the
pride and glory of English letters. It will take

a more vigorous logic than Primrose Criticism employs to set aside the verdict of this splendid array of scholars.

It may strengthen the confidence of the wavering to glance at some of the allusions made to Shakespeare in connection with the play of 'Richard III.' by contemporaneous and immediately succeeding 'poets. There does not seem to have been a suspicion in Shakespeare's day that he was not the author of this tragedy, or that he had perpetrated the literary fraud of putting his name to a drama which he did not write.

One of the earliest references to Shakespeare is made in John Weever's Poem (1599), *Ad Gulielmum Shakespeare.*

" Honie-Tong'd *Shakespeare* when I saw thine issue
I swore *Apollo* got them and none other."

Of this " issue," the poet mentions " Rose-checkt *Adonis,*" " Faire fire-hot *Venus,*" " Chaste *Lucretia,*" and

" *Romeo-Richard ;* more whose names I know not."

Francis Meres, in his ' Palladis Tamia,' 1598, refers to Shakespeare in the words : —

" As Plautus and Seneca are accounted the best for Comedy and Tragedy among the

Latins; so Shakespeare among ye English is the
most excellent in both kinds of the stage . . .
witness . . . for Tragedy his Richard the 2,
Richard the 3, Henry the 4, King John, Titus
Andronicus and his Romeo and Juliet."

There was a rather broad anecdote current
in Shakespeare's time, in which both the poet's
and the actor Burbage's names were associated
with the name and play of 'Richard III.,'
which would be out of character here. But this
same Burbage, Shakespeare's friend and the
original Richard, is introduced as one of the
characters in a play entitled 'The Returne
from Pernassus ; or the Scourge of Simony,
publiquely acted by the Students in St. John's
College in Camebridge, 1606.' The following
lines occur in this play : —

"*Kemp.* Few of the university pen plaies well,
they smell too much of that writer *Ovid*, and that
writer *Metamorphosis*, and talke too much of *Pro-
serpina* & *Juppiter*. Why here 's our fellow *Shakespeare* puts them all downe, I, and *Ben Jonson*, too.
O, that *Ben Jonson* is a pestilent fellow, he brought
up *Horace* giving the Poets a pill, but our fellow
Shakespeare hath given him a purge that made him
beray his credit.

.   .   .   .

Burbage. I like your face, and the proportion of
your body for Richard the 3. I pray, M. Phil. let me
see you act a little of it.

Philo. Now is the winter of our discontent,
Made glorious summer by this sonne of Yorke," etc·

In a religious poem on 'Saint Mary Mag-
dalen's Conversion,' written by 'C. J.,' 1603,
the following lines occur : —

" Of *Helens* rape and *Troyes* besieged Towne,
Of Troylus faith, and *Cressids* falsitie,
Of *Richards* stratagems for the english crowne,
Of *Tarquins* lust, and Lucrece chastitie,
Of these, of none of these my muse now treates,
Of greater conquests, warres and loves she speakes."

Richard Brathwaite, in 'A Strappado for the
Devill,' 1615, writes the lines : —

" If I had liv'd but in King Richard's days,
Who in his heat of passion, midst the force
Of his assailants troubled many waies,
Crying A horse, a kingdome for a horse,
O ! then my horse, which now at livery stayes,
Had beene set free, where now he 's forc't to stand,
And like to fall into the Ostler's hand."

If it be kept in mind that these allusions
to Shakespeare and his 'Richard III.' were
made in his own lifetime and during the time
in which Burbage was gaining celebrity as the
principal character in the tragedy, the state-
ment that Shakespeare was credited with the
authorship of 'Richard III.,' and that this

tragedy produced a deep impression on literary as well as vulgar minds, will be admitted.

John Milton was one of Shakespeare's most
enthusiastic eulogists, and, beyond question, an
ardent student of his works. It would be remarkable for him to have given special attention to 'Richard III.' without discovering that
it was written in a style wholly foreign to the
manner of Shakespeare, if such were the case.
It is matter for wonder that Milton's poetic
tastes, instincts, and judgment did not equal
the Primrose sense of Peter Bell in detecting
the un-Shakespearian character of that tragedy. It is still more surprising, if the play is
so very commonplace and is not the production of Shakespeare's genius, that glorious
John Milton should have found in that very
play some of the most striking ideas which he
has introduced into 'Paradise Lost,' and that
he should have quoted from that very play in
his prose works, where he attributes the play
to Shakespeare. Sir William Blackstone and
Edmund Malone could not but think that
Milton was indebted for his characterization
of Satan to these lines : —

" Sin, death, and hell have set their marks on him ;
And all their ministers attend on him."

ACT I. *Scene* 3.

In ' Eikonoklastes,' written in answer to
' Eikon Basilike,' in 1690, Milton makes this
striking reference to Shakespeare and the
play of ' Richard III. : ' —

" From Stories of this nature both Ancient
and Modern which abound, the Poets also, and
some English, have been in this Point so mind-
ful of *Decorum*, as to put never more pious
words in the Mouth of any Person, than of a
Tyrant. I shall not instance an abstruse
Author, wherein the King may be less conver-
sant, but one whom we well know was the
Closet Companion of these his Solitudes, *William Shakespeare;* who introduces the Person
of *Richard* the Third, speaking, in as high a
strain of Piety, and mortification, as is uttered
in any passage of this Book and sometimes to
the same sense and purpose with some words
in this Place, I *intended,* saith he, *not only
to oblige my Friends, but mine enemies.* The
like saith *Richard, Act* II. *Scene* I : —

> ' *I do not know that English Man alive,*
> *With whom my soul is any jot at odds,*
> *More than the Infant that is born to-night;*
> *I thank my God for my humility.*'

" Other stuff of this sort may be read throughout the whole Tragedy, wherein the Poet us'd
not much License in departing from the Truth
of History, which delivers him a deep Dissembler, not of his affections only, but of Religion."

As the great poets themselves, including
Jonson, Milton, Dryden, and Pope, never
questioned the Shakespearian authorship of
'Richard III.,' so the great actors who have
won their renown in Shakespearian characters, and who have made Richard III. one
of the most celebrated histrionic representations of the English stage, have never
detected that Richard was not Shakespeare's.
Burbage, Ryan, Cibber, Garrick, Mossop,
Henderson, Cooke, Kean, Kemble, Booth,
Macready — all the great, original Richards
— have had as firm confidence in the Shakespearian authorship of this character as they
have had of Hamlet, Macbeth, Coriolanus,
Othello, Shylock, or Lear. It is ordinarily,
if not extraordinarily reasonable, to suppose that actors of such intelligence and
genius, actors devoted to the study and
representation of Shakespeare, would be
able to detect, if it existed, the un-Shakespearian character of 'Richard III.' The
universal opinion of the stage is not easily
to be set aside by the Primrose Criticism.
Peter Bell has not a more authoritative
voice than Burbage, Betterton, Cibber, Garrick, Kemble, Cooke, Kean, Young, and
Macready.

The judgment of learned and philosophical students of Shakespeare should not be ig-
nored in a discussion of this character. Yet
Primrose Criticism is peculiarly and significantly hostile to anything that approaches the
uncommon in sense, learning, scholarship, or
subtlety of criticism ; hence its antipathy to
German criticism, and the scientific, philosophical instincts of the German mind. There
may be method in this madness when Shakespeare is under discussion, as it is beyond all
dispute that the Germans are the broadest,
profoundest, and most scholarly critics and
commentators of Shakespeare in the world.
Englishmen must admit this, as the able and
candid Furnivall has done.   Lessing, Goethe,
Schiller, Tieck, Schlegel, Ulrici, and Gervinus
are names that cannot be cast into shadow
by even such names as Pope, Dryden, Johnson, Malone, Steevens, Collier, and Halliwell-
Phillipps.   If these open-eyed German critics
see more in the primrose than the littleness
and inferiority of it, so do they also see more
in the dramatic delineation of the character
of Richard III. than the second-rate genius
of a Marlowe, a Peele, or a Greene.

Schiller, with a true anti-Primrose spirit,
closed his reading of ' Richard III.' with the

splendid encomium : "It is one of the sub-
limest tragedies I know." Ulrici finds in
' Richard III.' the fifth act of the great
tragedy of which ' Richard II.' is the first.
In a very un-Primrose fashion, this philoso-
pher makes bold to say : —

" No drama shows more distinctly than Henry
VI. and its continuation Richard III. how the
two sides of tragedy and comedy — according
to their ethical significance — meet in the historical drama, and become blended into a higher
unity."

Schlegel advances a similar theory, and implies the Shakespearian authorship of ' Richard
III.' when he says : —

" These four plays ['Henry VI.' and ' Richard III.'] were undoubtedly composed in succession, as is proved by the style and the spirit
in the handling of the subject : the last is defi-
nitely announced in the one which precedes it,
and is also full of references to it ; the same
views run through the series ; in a word, the
whole make together only one single work."

This distinguished scholar thinks that the Englishmen's great admiration of this tragedy " is
certainly in every respect well founded."

Dr. Gervinus, in his 'Shakespeare Commentaries,' unconsciously arrays himself against all Primrose Criticism when he bluntly and confidently says, with the assurance of a scholar : —

" Richard III. is Shakespeare's first tragedy of undoubted personal authorship ; it is written in connection with Henry VI., and appears as its direct continuation."

But the great Professor comes into still closer collision with the Primrose Criticism when he says : —

" Richard III. shows extraordinary progress when compared to Henry VI. . . . The poetic diction, however much it reminds us of Henry VI., has gained surprisingly in finish, richness, and truth ; we need only compare the words of Anne at the beginning (Act I. Sc. 2) with the best parts of Henry VI., to find how thoroughly they are animated with the breath of passion, how pure and natural is their flow, and how entirely the expression is but the echo of the feeling."

It would seem that Primrose Criticism had involved itself in a vastly greater iconoclastic enterprise than it had bargained for, in its attempt to disprove the Shakespearian authorship of ' Richard III.,' since scientific criticism

demands that the genuineness of all these related historical plays be invalidated together,
or that they all stand together in their unquestioned integrity.

Attention is further called to the reasons
laid down by the Primrose Criticism for robbing Shakespeare of his ' Richard III.'

It is asserted that the tragedy is not written
in Shakespeare's style ; that it proceeds with
a different gait ; that it contains nonsense and
defective metre ; that it is devoid of humor
and eloquence ; and that it contains whole
scenes where the author's mind seems at
dead low-tide throughout, and lays bare all
its shallows and its ooze.   With these serious
charges made against the tragedy, singularly
enough, not a shadow of a proof, not even an
illustration or a quotation, is given in support
of the charges.

It may again be suggested that it is remarkable that men of the poetical tastes of Jonson,
Milton, Dryden, Pope, Schiller and Goethe ;
and men of the critical acuteness and ripe
scholarship of Johnson, Steevens, Malone,
Hazlitt, Lamb, Halliwell-Phillipps, and Richard
Grant White ; and men of the splendid histrionic genius of Burbage, Garrick, Cooke,
Kean, Kemble, and Macready, have not de-

tected the un-Shakespearian style, the alien,
unknown, and vulgar gait of this remarkable
' Richard III.'

As to the "nonsense," it would be un-
Shakespearian if it were absolutely free from it.
The same is true of the " defective metre."
If Sophocles, Æschylus, Corneille, Racine, or
Voltaire were to be our model, then Shakespeare would be full of " nonsense." The
violation or utter ignoring of the Unities, the
trampling under foot of Aristotelian rules of
dramatic composition, would be considered
" nonsense " by the classical school. But if
this be the " nonsense " for which ' Richard
III.' is condemned, then must many a play of
Shakespeare's come under the ban of con-
demnation. Nor is this the only kind of
" nonsense " that may be found in Shakespeare's plays. Ben Jonson made this charge
in his day : —

" His wit was in his owne power ; would the
rule of it had beene so too. Many times hee
fell into those things, could not escape laughter :
As when hee said in the person of *Cæsar*, one
speaking to him : ' *Cæsar thou dost me wrong.*'
Hee replyed : ' *Cæsar did never wrong, but
with just cause :* ' and such like ; which were
ridiculous. But he redeemed his vices, with
his vertues."

3

Anachronisms are "nonsense" to those who measure by the classical standards ; but if such "nonsense" is un-Shakespearian, — and none would seem greater to Aristotle, Ben Jonson, or Voltaire, — then must nearly every play of Shakespeare's be denied its accredited merit and high origin.

'Coriolanus' is marred and disfigured by the "nonsense" of Titus Lartius quoting Cato's estimate of a true soldier, when Cato was not born until two hundred and fifty years after the time in which Lartius mentions him. In the same play Menenius Agrippa refers to Alexander the Great, more than two hundred years before the conqueror of the world was born. And the same person speaks of "the most sovereign prescription in Galen," six hundred and fifty years before the great physician saw the light of day.

In the tragedy of 'Hamlet' we are astonished to hear Hamlet and the King in the tenth or eleventh century speak of the school at Wittenberg, which was not founded until 1502. Then reference is therein made to a performance of the play of 'Julius Cæsar,' which took place at the Oxford University in 1582 ! Several references are made to "brazen

cannon " which were not in existence in
Hamlet's time.   Here is " nonsense " !

In 'Merry Wives of Windsor,' one may
be surfeited with "nonsense."   What right
has Bardolph, in 1400, to know anything
about "three German devils, three Doctor
Faustuses"?   What sense is there in Shallow's
threatening Falstaff with, " I will make a Star-
Chamber matter of it," when the Star-Chamber
Court was not in existence?   Mill sixpences
were first coined in 1561, and the " Edward
shovel-boards" not earlier than about 1550 ;
yet Slender accuses Pistol, in 1400, of picking
his pocket and robbing him "of seven groats
of mill sixpences, and two Edward shovel-
boards."   Mrs. Ford, in a most unaccount-
able fashion, seemed to be familiar with the
tune of "Green Sleeves" one hundred and
seventy-five years before it was composed,
which was in 1580.   And Mr. Page had heard
that "the Frenchman hath good skill in his
rapier," nearly two hundred years before the
rapier was introduced.

In the 'Winter's Tale' is the famous "nonsense" which provoked the ridicule of Ben
Jonson, to which Drummond refers : —

" He said that Shakespeare wanted art, and
sometimes sense ; for in one of his plays he

brought in a number of men, saying they had
suffered shipwreck in Bohemia, where is no
sea near by 100 miles."

To any sense but Primrose-sense it seems
" nonsense " for one to put into a drama such
a dialogue as this : —

> "*Ant.* Thou art perfect then, our ship hath touch'd
> upon
> The deserts of Bohemia ?
> *Mar.*   Ay, my lord."

In ' Henry VI.' mention is made of Machi-
avel, who was but two years old when Henry
VI. died.

It has been charged that it is " nonsense "
for the dramatist to represent Fortinbras, in
the tragedy of ' Hamlet,' as appearing at a
certain time in Denmark, and in an hour
and a half returning victorious from Poland.
And it is equal " nonsense " to represent
Othello as passing from Venice to Cyprus
in a few moments of time.

All that Bowdler eliminated from the text of
Shakespeare — " those words and expressions
. . . which cannot with Propriety be read
aloud in a Family " — must be branded as
" nonsense." The mixing up of tragedy and
comedy in the same play is, by some, considered " nonsense." It would indeed be diffi-

cult to mention a species of "nonsense" that
may not be found in Shakespeare. But there
is hardly one of his plays that has less "nonsense" in it than 'Richard III.' This is true,
whether the "nonsense" be the "nonsense"
of vulgarity, of historical inaccuracy, of un-
naturalness, or of the violation of the Unities
of time and place. And the very criticism
which would on the Primrose basis rob Shakespeare of 'Richard III.' would rob him of
nearly every one of his great creations.

It may be of interest to take at least a
glance at the suggestion that Shakespeare was
so perfect in his poetic art that he could not
have written in faulty style, nor in violation
of any poetical canon. It is well known that
he was admired by his contemporaries and
immediate successors as a natural genius rather
than as a trained and scholarly artist.

Ben Jonson, who knew Shakespeare per-
sonally, was candid in saying : "Shakespeare
wanted Art. . . . His wit was in his owne
power; would the rule of it had been so too."

Good Thomas Fuller expressed the common sentiment of the seventeenth century
when he wrote of Shakespeare : —

"He was an eminent instance of the truth
of that rule, '*Poeta non fit, sed nascitur;*' one

is not *made*, but born a poet. Indeed his learning was very little, so that, as *Cornish diamonds* are not polished by any Lapidary, but are pointed and smoothed even as they are taken out of the earth, so *Nature* itself was all the *Art* which was used upon him."

Berkenhead, in praising Beaumont and Fletcher, most justly said : —

" Brave Shakespeare flow'd, yet had his Ebbings too,
Often above Himselfe, sometimes below."

Milton, master of poetic art, with taste and instinct exquisite, implies Shakespeare's deficiency in art as he listens to

"sweetest Shakespeare, Fancy's child,
Warble his native wood-notes wild."

Dryden honestly says of his idol : —

" I cannot say he is everywhere alike ; were he so, I should do him injury to compare him with the greatest of mankind. He is many times flat, insipid ; his comic wit degenerating into clinches, his serious swelling into bombast."

As compared with Jonson, this is Dryden's estimate of Shakespeare : —

" The *faultless* Johnson *equally* writ well ;
Shakespeare made *faults*, but then did more excel."

Again this noble writer says : —

" Shakespeare, who many times has written better than any poet, in any language, is yet so far from writing wit *always*, or expressing that wit according to the dignity of the subject, that he writes, in many places, below the dullest writer of ours, or any precedent age."

Edward Phillips, the nephew of Milton, in his ' Theatrum Poetarum,' 1675, says : —

" Shakespeare, in spight of all his unfiled expressions, his rambling and indigested fancys, the laughter of the Critical, yet must be confessed a *poet* above many that go beyond him in Literature some degree."

And again : —

" From an Actor of Tragedies and Comedies he became a *Maker ;* and such a *Maker*, that though some others may perhaps pretend to a more exact *Decorum* and *œconomie*, especially in Tragedy, never any express'd a more lofty and tragic height ; never any represented nature more purely to the life, and where the polishments of Art are most wanting, as probably his Learning was not extraordinary, he pleaseth with a certain *wild* and *native* Elegance."

Pope, with most excellent judgment, wrote in his preface : —

" It must be owned, that with all these great excellencies, he has almost as great defects ;

and that as he has certainly written better, so he has perhaps written worse, than any other."

Samuel Johnson made bold to ascribe certain faults to Shakespeare, by saying : —

" The style of Shakespeare was in itself ungrammatical, perplexed and obscure."

The criticisms quoted above apply to the nonsense, the faulty style, the defective metre, and the occasional commonplace passages to be found in Shakespeare's works.

From these criticisms the conclusion is to be drawn that, contrary to the opinion of the Primrose Criticism, Shakespeare wrote nonsense and indulged in defective metre. And this further conclusion is logical, that to reject the Shakespearian authorship of ' Richard III.' on the ground that it contains nonsense and defective metre, would warrant the rejection of nearly every play ascribed to Shakespeare. The faults of 'Richard III.' are not un-Shakespearian. And, with Professor Richardson, all may admit that "this tragedy, *like every work* of Shakespeare, has many faults."

It is further implied in the Primrose Criticism that as ' Richard III.' is without humor it lacks one of the infallible characteristics of

Shakespearian method and genius. Perhaps
no play of this original dramatist adheres more
closely to the classical standard with regard to
its tragical unity than 'Richard III.' It lacks,
let it be admitted, the unclassical admixture of
comedy. But the play is of such an intensely
cruel and tragic nature that it could with less
consistency than any other play admit of the
introduction of a comic strain. Its very diabolism seems to forbid any relief to the horror,
or the admission of any ray of jest or clownish-
ness into the damnable darkness. If, however,
by the term "humor" we may include the idea
of wit, sarcasm, cunning and adroit play of
words, then, certainly, one of the greatest, if
grimmest, humorists of Shakespeare's creation
is Richard III. There are lines in the first
soliloquy that contain humor. Gloster's wooing of Lady Anne, even in the presence of the
corpse of Henry VI., is not only most eloquent,
but consummately witty, bordering at least on
the humorous. The strawberry subterfuge by
which the Bishop of Ely is politely invited
out of the council in the Tower, is a cheerful
incident, if nothing more.

Nevertheless, it is true that this picture is
very sparingly relieved of its sombre character
by the comical or even by the humorous.

This fact, however, cannot rob the tragedy of
its Shakespearian character, which is determined by its positive rather than by its nega-
tive elements, by what it contains rather than
by what it lacks. A few of the great actors
have so studied this play as to find in it rays
of light, and in their acting they have relieved
the play of the monotonous horror by bring-
ing out the wit and even humor which they
found therein. Kemble, Cooke, and Kean in
particular were credited with the ability to
find and to set forth these features of the dark
tragedy. It was with difficulty that they
succeeded.

On what grounds the Primrose Criticism
insinuates that 'Richard III.' reveals a lack
of patriotism in its author it is difficult to determine. If to portray reckless, heartless, in-
satiable ambition, a love of power which
tramples underfoot the laws of God and so-
ciety, — if to hold up to the universal gaze for
everlasting execration

" That foul defacer of God's handy-work ;
That excellent grand tyrant of the earth," —

if to record with dramatic force the diabolical intrigues, and the final, just calamities
and ruin of a royal assassin and red-handed
usurper, — be unpatriotic, then Shakespeare

has indeed most successfully and commend-
ably proven himself of an unpatriotic spirit. If
patriotism means simply loyalty to a " House "
or an administration rather than to the country, then of that narrow sort of patriotism
Shakespeare, the author of ' Richard III.,'
was not largely and conspicuously possessed.
But that great tragedy was written by a pen
which had been inspired with the loftiest patriotism, — a love of country and the rights of
men. The spirit that wrote the play breathes
in the patriotic prayer of Richmond : —

" O, now, let Richmond and Elizabeth,
  The true succeeders of each royal house,
  By God's fair ordinance conjoin together !
  And let their heirs (God, if thy will be so)
  Enrich the time to come with smooth-faced peace,
  With smiling plenty, and fair prosperous days !
  Abate the edge of traitors, gracious Lord,
  That would reduce these bloody days again,
  And make poor England weep in streams of blood !
  Let them not live to taste this land's increase,
  That would with treason wound this fair land's
     peace !
  Now civil wounds are stopp'd, peace lives again ;
  That she may long live here, God say — Amen ! "

Primrose Criticism insinuates that to admit
the Shakespearian authorship of this play
would be to accuse the poet of therein per-
mitting his mind to remain " at dead low-tide,

and lay bare all its shallows and its ooze." It
is difficult for one to understand Schiller's admiration of such a shallow and oozy-minded
tragedy. And if these lines are at a poetic
and dramatic " dead low-tide," what was
" Marlowe's mighty line," when such a scholarly critic as Chalmers, in turning from Marlowe's play, must say : —

" Certain it is that when we open Shakespeare's Richard III. we seem to mount from
the uniform flat, wherein we had been travelling
with uncheered steps, to an exalted eminence,
from whence we behold around us, an extensive
country, diversified by hill and dale, refreshed
by many waters, and traversed by roads, leading to hospitable mansions :

' *Glos.* Now is the winter of our discontent
Made glorious summer by this sun of York.' "

No " low-tide " performance here, to the
mind of the Scotch antiquarian and critic !

All men have not been able to detect the
shallows and ooze which the Primrose Criticism seems to find in ' Richard III.' Hazlitt
had certainly seen virtues in this tragedy
which escaped the eye of Peter Bell, for he
wrote : —

" The play itself is undoubtedly a very powerful effusion of Shakespeare's genius. The

groundwork of the character of Richard — that mixture of intellectual vigour with moral depravity, in which Shakespeare delighted to show his strength — gave full scope as well as temptation to the exercise of his imagination."

Coleridge must have found great excellences in this play; and his keen, critical eye must have overlooked the "shallows" and "ooze," else he could not have written : —

"Shakespeare here, as in all his great parts, develops in a tone of sublime morality the dreadful consequences of placing the moral in subordination to the mere intellectual being."

Let it not be supposed that an attempt is here made to prove the superiority of 'Richard III.' to all other Shakespearian productions. As a literary work it cannot hold rank with 'Hamlet,' 'Othello,' 'Lear,' and many other plays of this poet. Some may even wonder, with Johnson, Steevens, and Malone, why it has been so universally admired, without doubting its Shakespearian origin.

Hazlitt pronounces 'Richard III.' a play for the stage rather than for the study. Others criticise it for its inadaptability to the stage. Possibly the Cibber adaptation of the play was better calculated to produce theatrical effect than the original, but there can be no question that the 'Richard III.' of Shakespeare is the more perfect and admirable in the study. Indeed, the Cibber adaptation eliminates portions which, in the study and from the literary standpoint, are the finest portions of the play, and rank with the noblest and most elegant poetic strains of Shakespeare.

That which would be "dead low-tide," "shallows," "ooze," to the play-goer and to the actor, might be high-tide, ocean deeps, crystalline purity of philosophic thought and poetic form to the student and moralist.

Let it be admitted that some of the scenes and dialogues would be tedious and devoid of good taste and exciting interest on the stage; the same admission must be made touching many of Shakespeare's plays. If this fault is un-Shakespearian, surely there is hardly a purely Shakespearian play in existence. There are entire plays of Shakespeare which have never been popular on the stage, and quite a large number of them have entirely disappeared from the repertoire of the Shakespearian actors. Who of this generation has witnessed a successful and popular performance of 'Timon of Athens,' 'Pericles,' 'Ti-

tus Andronicus,' 'Cymbeline,' 'King John,'
'Henry VI.,' 'Troilus and Cressida,' 'Measure
for Measure'?

But the drama is not to be judged and
fashioned by the tastes and demands of the
theatre alone. Doubtless many have agreed
with Charles Lamb that Shakespeare cannot
be acted, that the stage is not great enough
for his dramatic creations. The theatre demanded that the original tragedy of 'Richard
III.' should be changed; the change was
made, and the play thereby gained popularity
for the time being on the stage, but lost popularity in the study.

Colley Cibber almost destroyed the literary
identity of the great tragedy when in 1700 he
adapted it to the stage; yet he made the character of Richard, whose horrible identity he
preserved, a great favorite with actors and
play-goers. And though Garrick, Cooke, and
Kean achieved fame in the performance of
this mutilated play, who will say that Shakespeare, in *revisiting* "the glimpses of the
moon," would be willing to adopt the "adaptation" and applaud Cibber for his pains?
Who will acknowledge from the standpoint of
literary dramatic criticism that the Cibber
adaptation is equal to the original drama?

Now the argument is this, that a dramatic composition may be of high excellence from a literary and intellectual standpoint which on the stage, from an actor's or the auditor's point, would prove too intricate, obscure, tame, or even revolting. Such a play, however, does not necessarily reveal the "shallows" and "ooze" and "dead lowtide" of its author's mind ; it may show the greater heights, depths, powers, and splendors of it.

Astonishment increases when this new Primrose Criticism makes the remarkable discovery that 'Richard III." is devoid of eloquence, and is not therefore of Shakespearian origin. It must be a very uncommon taste that is deaf to the eloquence of Richard's soliloquies, of Clarence's dream, of Margaret's curses, of Richmond's orations and prayers. Did not Gloster woo Lady Anne most eloquently? What can exceed the beauty and pathos of Edward's eulogy of his brother?

"*K. Edw.* Have I a tongue to doom my brother's
    death,
And shall that tongue give pardon to a slave?
My brother kill'd no man, his fault was thought,
And yet his punishment was bitter death.
Who sued to me for him? who, in my wrath,
Kneel'd at my feet, and bade me be advis'd?

Who spoke of brotherhood? who spoke of love?
Who told me, how the poor soul did forsake
The mighty Warwick, and did fight for me?
Who told me, in the field at Tewksbury,
When Oxford had me down, he rescu'd me,
And said, *Dear brother, live, and be a king?*
Who told me, when we both lay in the field,
Frozen almost to death, how he did lap me
Even in his garments; and did give himself,
All thin and naked, to the numb-cold night?
All this from my remembrance brutish wrath
Sinfully pluck'd, and not a man of you
Had so much grace to put it in my mind.
But when your carters or your waiting-vassals
Have done a drunken slaughter, and defac'd
The precious image of our dear Redeemer,
You straight are on your knees for pardon, pardon;
And I, unjustly too, must grant it you : —
But for my brother, not a man would speak, —
Nor I (ungracious) speak unto myself
For him, poor soul. — The proudest of you all
Have been beholden to him in his life;
Yet none of you would once plead for his life. —
O God! I fear, thy justice will take hold
On me, and you, and mine, and yours, for this. —
Come, Hastings, help me to my closet. O, poor
    Clarence ! "

Is such an eloquence unworthy of Shakespeare's pen?

In reading Queen Elizabeth's farewell to
the Tower which holds "those tender babes,"
and in reading Tyrrel's description of the
"ruthless butchery," one joins with Hazlitt in

4

pronouncing them "some of those wonderful bursts of feeling, done to the life, to the
very height of fancy and nature, which our
Shakespeare alone could give."

Has ever an actor in the noble character of
Richmond doubted that he was pronouncing an eloquence equal to that of Henry V.
before Harfleur, when on famous Bosworth
field he harangued his troops, closing with
the spirited and thrilling words : —

" Then, in the name of God, and all these rights,
  Advance your standards, draw your willing swords :
  For me, the ransom of my bold attempt
  Shall be this cold corpse on the earth's cold face ;
  But if I thrive, the gain of my attempt
  The least of you shall share his part thereof.
  Sound, drums and trumpets, boldly and cheerfully ;
  God, and Saint George ! Richmond, and victory ! "

Not only the actions, but the very words of
Richard on that fatal field were eloquent : —

" Fight, gentlemen of England ! fight, bold yeomen !
  Draw, archers, draw your arrows to the head !
  Spur your proud horses hard, and ride in blood ;
  Amaze the welkin with your broken staves ! "

" A thousand hearts are great within my bosom :
  Advance our standards, set upon our foes ;
  Our ancient word of courage, fair Saint George,
  Inspire us with the spleen of fiery dragons !
  Upon them ! Victory sits on our helms."

As Garrick acted the part, throwing into it
the highest spirit of gallantry, what stirring
eloquence was Richard's in the scene : —

> " *K. Rich.* A horse ! a horse ! my kingdom for a
> horse !
> *Catesby.* Withdraw, my lord, I'll help you to a
> horse.
> *K. Rich.* Slave, I have set my life upon a cast,
> And I will stand the hazard of the die ;
> I think, there be six Richmonds in the field ;
> Five have I slain to-day, instead of him : —
> A horse ! a horse ! my kingdom for a horse ! "

If eloquence be the test, ' Richard III.' is
Shakespeare's.

The Primrose Criticism cannot suppress its
mirth at the appearance of the ghosts on
Bosworth field, and intimates that the scene
is unworthy of Shakespeare, and hence was
not his creation. Why Peter Bell does not
laugh at the whole tribe of dramatic ghosts
and every other sort of ghosts, is not apparent.

The ghosts in ' Hamlet,' ' Macbeth,' and
' Julius Cæsar ' are as open to criticism, and
are as provocative of mirth as the ghosts in
' Richard III.' Why Banquo's ghost should
appear to Macbeth, and the ghost of the
Royal Dane to Hamlet, and the ghost of
Cæsar to Brutus, without challenging the

criticism of Peter Bell, while the appearance
of the ghosts of Richard's victims on Bosworth field should be thought laughable, is
perhaps unworthy of serious inquiry. Whether
any ghost scene be pleasing or not to the
reader of this age, there is a seriousness of
mind in which to study the dramatic requirements and necessities of an earlier age,
which the Primrose Criticism does not seem
to cultivate. There is at least a philosophical
dignity, which should ever accompany criticism, to be found in Schlegel's remarks
on the ghost scene in ' Richard III.' In
explanation of Richard's heroic death, he
says : —

" He fights at last against Richmond like a
desperado, and dies the honorable death of a
hero on the field of battle. Shakespeare could
not change this historical issue, and yet it is by
no means satisfactory to our moral feelings, as
Lessing, when speaking of a German play on
the same subject, has very judiciously remarked.
How has Shakespeare solved this difficulty?
By a wonderful invention he opens a prospect
into the other world, and shows us Richard in
his last moments already branded with the stamp
of reprobation. We see Richard and Richmond in the night before the battle sleeping in
their tents : the spirits of the murdered victims

of the tyrant ascend in succession, and pour out their curses against him, and their blessings on his adversary. These apparitions are properly but the dreams of the two generals represented visibly. It is no doubt contrary to probability that their tents should only be separated by so small a space; but Shakespeare could reckon on poetical spectators who were ready to take the breadth of the stage for the distance between two hostile camps, if for such indulgence they were to be recompensed by beauties of so sublime a nature as this series of spectres and Richard's awakening soliloquy. The catastrophe of Richard the Third is, in respect to the external event, very like that of Macbeth; we have only to compare the thorough difference of handling them to be convinced that Shakespeare has most accurately observed poetical justice in the genuine sense of the word, that is, as signifying the relation of an invisible blessing or curse which hangs over human sentiments and actions."

It is certainly refreshing to turn from the Primrose sneer to such a philosophical criticism as this, which, if it serve no other end, may suggest the value of German seriousness above much American flippancy.

But why should Shakespeare be ridiculed for dramatizing tradition and history? The subject matter of the ghost scene was not

invented by Shakespeare. The dramatist
could not eliminate that part of Richard's
experience. The historians told it all before
the poet adapted it to the stage. The horrible dreams, the appearance of ghosts and
even devils to the tormented mind of Richard
on the eve of battle, are in the records. Let
the Primrose Criticism attempt to dramatize
this experience less ludicrously ; let it under-
take to do it more grandly and impressively.

Any criticism that overlooks the principal
character of a drama must be logically defective if not scientifically worthless, however
charmingly and elegantly it may be presented.
Where criticism contents itself with pointing
out the mote that dances in the beam of
light, the withered leaf that hangs on the
branch of the oak, the broken feather that
still clings to the pinion of the eagle, the
stain on the sail of the noble ship, the spot
on the face of the glorious sun, the justice
of the method may be seriously questioned.
One of the most remarkable exhibitions of
criticism ever witnessed was the recent notable Primrose study of the play of ' Richard III.' with Richard left out. Defective
metre ; poverty of style ; lack of eloquence,
humor, and patriotism ; superfluity of ghost ;

intellectual " dead low-tide," " shallows,"
" ooze ; " and deliberate nonsense, — were
dwelt upon with elegance and subtlety of
assertion ; but what of the character Richard III. ? Nothing, absolutely nothing ! And
yet there is no other play of Shakespearian
authorship that is so completely concentrated
in one character as this. There is no other character that has become popular for the stage in
which all the interests of the tragedy in which
it is cast centre so completely. The play of
' Richard III.' leaves stamped upon the imagination and memory but one impression —
Richard.

In a study of Shakespeare's other tragedies
we find, for instance, that Hamlet, Othello,
and Macbeth severally share with one or two
other characters the interest of the play in
which they appear. But Richard is himself
alone. He is the whole play. And as he
would not share the honors of the kingdom
with another, but tyrannically demanded all
and all the power usurped ; so will he not
share the interest of a dramatic plot with another : the play is his, the stage is his, as the
kingdom is his alone. " Richard is the soul,
or rather the dæmon, of the whole tragedy."
However defective the metre, however lame

the style, however tame the dialogue in certain parts, however dreary and even revolting some of the events and scenes in this tragedy, there stands a character which no pen but Shakespeare's could have delineated.

The most characteristic quality of Shakespeare's plays is the wonderful, unparalleled delineation of character to be found in them. Shakespeare was pre-eminent in his power " to hold, as 'twere, the mirror up to nature ; to show virtue her own feature, scorn her own image, and the very age and body of the time his form and pressure." It is not the metre of the tragedy of ' Hamlet ' that distinguishes it, and secures the immortality of its popularity, but the delineation of the character of Hamlet. It is not the absence of " nonsense," but the character of Shylock, that keeps up the world's interest in the ' Merchant of Venice.' It is not the literary style of the play of ' King Lear ' that has placed it above all other modern tragedies ; that is accomplished by the character of Lear. Neither the " patriotism " nor the " humor " of ' Macbeth,' but the character of Macbeth himself, as therein set forth, makes the tragedy great in literature and on the stage. So is it with the tragedy of ' Richard III. ; ' it is

great because therein the characterization of
Richard is great. No dramatic person that
Shakespeare's mighty pen ever drew is more
worthy of his genius. No character has won
greater fame and .popularity on the stage.
No character, with the possible exception of
Lear, demands in its representation the exercise of greater histrionic genius. There have
been but four great Richards on the English
stage, and they are the acknowledged greatest
geniuses of the stage. If another hand than
Shakespeare's drew this wonderful character,
then let not Greene, Marlowe, Jonson, or
Fletcher share the fame of the "Bard of
Avon," but let the unknown author and creator of 'Richard III.' be partner in the pos-
session of the greatest fame in dramatic
literature.

Are we certain that Swift wrote the 'Tale
of a Tub,' and Scott 'The Antiquary,' because nobody else could do it? Then Shakespeare drew the dramatic character of Richard
III. because nobody else could do it. Yes,
"there is a gait that marks the mind as well
as the body;" and if not in the metre nor
the literary style, in the great, impressive, terrible character of Richard III. may be detected the infallible, unmistakable mental gait

of Shakespeare. It is submitted whether the Shakespearian character of any play in question is not to be determined rather from a study of the persons than of the prosody of the play.

Primrose Criticism will condescendingly admit that Shakespeare may have adapted the play to the stage, "making additions sometimes longer, sometimes shorter." But let it be noticed that the true author of the original play is not mentioned. No attempt is made to prove that the play had an existence in literature before 1597, when Shakespeare published it. Primrose Criticism is not wanting in antiquarian knowledge ; let it therefore mention for the world's information just the play, with its title, date of publication, author's name, and dramatic plan, which Shakespeare laid his cunning if not thievish hand upon, and appropriated to himself. Will Primrose Criticism claim that it was Marlowe's play? or "A Tragical Report of King Richard, a Ballad," published in 1586? If so, there is an opportunity for candid comparison and argument.

George Steevens tells us — what many an antiquarian well knows — that several dramas on the present subject had been written before Shakespeare attempted it. If Shakespeare's attempt was not a new, an original, and a genuine production, then, in the name of critical fairness, it is unjust to charge Shakespeare with literary theft until it has been proven who else did write the play, or that it had a previous existence.

With all the poems and plays on this subject before them, after careful study and comparison, no editor, commentator, antiquarian, or critic has been able to find the original play or poem which Primrose Criticism accuses Shakespeare of stealing, revamping, and publishing in his own name. Common sense and common fairness suggest that there never existed such a play or poem, and that, until it is produced, Shakespeare is entitled to the honor and glory of having been the author of ' Richard III.'

That Shakespeare made his honey from the flowers that were blooming about him ; that he did not create the silk and gold which he wove into the rich tapestries of his fancy ; that he hewed from existing quarries the blocks out of which he constructed his gorgeous dramatic palaces, will be admitted. Not a play of his unquestioned authorship exists that does not bear proofs of his indebtedness to poets, historians, romancists, and translators, of his own and of preceding times. It is well known that there were already in existence and in common circulation the stories, poems, and chronicles which inspired or suggested the plots of Shakespeare's greatest plays. The stories of ' Hamlet,' ' Merchant of Venice,' ' Romeo and Juliet,' ' King Lear,' ' Macbeth,' ' Othello,' etc., were not original with Shakespeare ; they were only modified and dramatized by him. This is the work and mission of the dramatist. In such a sense the tragedy of ' Richard III.' was a dramatization of an historical time and person.

For the historical basis of this tragedy Shakespeare depended upon others. He did not evolve his historical plays from his internal consciousness. That he received suggestions from poets, novelists, and dramatists who had written upon the same subject, is as probable as that he obtained necessary information from sober and learned historians. But detecting Plutarch, Boccaccio, Sir Thomas More, Holinshed, Hall, Grafton, Painter, Florio, and other authors and translators, in the dramatic works of Shakespeare does not justify the insinuation that he was a plagiarist.

Nor will a scientific criticism attempt on such ground to base an argument for the un-Shakespearian character and style of 'Richard III.'

Having noticed what seem to be some of the defects of the Primrose Criticism in its discussion of the Shakespearian authorship of 'Richard III.' it may not be unprofitable for us to turn to a short study of the sources from which Shakespeare drew the subject-matter of his tragedy.

PART II.

THE HISTORICAL BASIS OF 'RICHARD III.'

"My villainy they have upon record."

THE HISTORICAL BASIS OF
RICHARD III.

GOETHE placed Shakespeare before
all other poets for power of invention
and for variety and originality of
characterization. Yet he knew that the dramatist seldom, if ever, invented the subject
matter of his plays. The jealousy of Greene
has not biassed the judgment of fair-minded
critics in determining Shakespeare's merit for
originality. The author of 'Groats-worth of
Wit' assailed Shakespeare after this fashion :

"There is an upstart Crow, beautified with
our feathers, that with his *Tygers heart wrapt
in a Players hide*, supposes he is well able to
bombast out a blanke verse as the best of you :
and being an absolute *Johannes factotum* is in
his owne conceit the onely Shake-scene in a
countrie. O, that I might entreate your rare wits

5

to be employed in more profitable courses : and
let those Apes imitate your past excellence, and
never more acquaint them with your admired
inventions."

It would take more than a groat's worth
of such wit to convince the world that the
'sweet Swan of Avon,' with borrowed or with
stolen wings, made

> " . . . those flights upon the banks of Thames
> That so did take Eliza and our James."

Few have had the temerity to charge Shakespeare with aping the excellences of superior
wits.   It was not necessary for that

> "Soule of the Age "

to depend upon the invention or originality
of any other genius of his time ;

> " Nature her selfe was proud of his designs,
> And joy'd to weare the dressing of his lines ! "

Though Shakespeare, in common with all
great dramatic poets, has borrowed the foundation material of his plays from history, fable,
classic lore, and romance, yet his power of
invention and his originality of genius are not
to be questioned.   His invention is shown,
not in the creation of the figures of his plays,

but in the elevation and transformation of them into poetic and dramatic characters. This, to the philosophical mind of Ulrici, " is proof of greater force and intensity of genius, greater truth and depth of intellect, than if he had himself invented the subject matter of his dramas."

For the subject matter of the historical tragedy of ' Richard III.,' Shakespeare was indebted to several sources, — historical and poetical. The principal sources were Holinshed, Grafton, Hall, Sir Thomas More, Marlowe, ' The True Tragedy of Richard III.,' and the ' Mirour for Magistrates.' If, as Walpole claims, the Shakespearian ' Richard ' is not true to historical facts, then the blame of it must lie at the door of the historian rather than of the dramatist. It is beyond question, that the world bases its conception of Richard's character on Shakespeare's play, and that the dramatist has done more than any other to prejudice the world's opinion to the theory of the unmitigated diabolism of this infamous tyrant and usurper. But it will be found that the historians approach Shakespeare in the darkness of their representations ; they approach him as nearly as sober, dispassionate history may approach impassioned drama.

The physical deformities of Richard, on which the poet makes him frequently soliloquize, both in ' Henry VI.' and ' Richard III.,' are minutely described by the historians. Several of the obscure or seemingly trifling passages of the play are suggested by Holinshed and More, and they appear in the play in almost the identical language of the historians. In illustration of these points reference is now made to the corresponding passages and descriptions found in the play, and the historical authorities on which the drama is based.

In the first soliloquy of Richard occur the lines : —

"But I, — that am not shap'd for sportive tricks,
   Nor made to court an amorous looking-glass;
   I, that am rudely stamp'd, and want love's majesty,
   To strut before a wanton ambling nymph;
   I, that am curtail'd of this fair proportion,
   Cheated of feature by dissembling nature,
   Deform'd, unfinish'd, sent before my time
   Into this breathing world, scarce half made up,
   And that so lamely and unfashionable,
   That dogs bark at me, as I halt by them ; —
   Why I, in this weak piping time of peace,
   Have no delight to pass away the time ;
   Unless to spy my shadow in the sun,
   And descant on mine own deformity."

After his wooing of Lady Anne he again refers to his bodily deformity : —

"And will she yet abase her eyes on me,
That cropp'd the golden prime of this sweet prince,
And made her widow to a woful bed ?
On me, whose all not equals Edward's moiety ?
On me, that halt, and am mis-shapen thus ? "

Lady Anne refers to Richard's physical condition when she cries : —

"Blush, blush, thou lump of foul deformity."

Again, spitting upon him and wishing her spittle were poison, she says : —

"Never hung poison on a fouler toad.
Out of my sight! thou dost infect mine eyes."

Queen Margaret's bitter curse contained the words : —

"Thou elvish-mark'd, abortive, rooting hog!
Thou that wast seal'd in thy nativity
The slave of nature, and the son of hell !
Thou slander of thy mother's heavy womb !
Thou loathed issue of thy father's loins !
Thou rag of honour ! "

Again she cries : —

" Sin, death, and hell, have set their marks on him."

In the third part of ' Henry VI.,' Gloster soliloquizes : —

"Why, love forswore me in my mother's womb;
And, for I should not deal in her soft laws,
She did corrupt frail nature with some bribe
To shrink mine arm up like a wither'd shrub;
To make an envious mountain on my back,
Where sits deformity to mock my body;
To shape my legs of an unequal size;
To disproportion me in every part,
Like to a chaos, or an unlick'd bear-whelp,
That carries no impression like the dam."

In the eyes of King Henry, Gloster was

" . . . . . an indigest deformed lump."

There seems to be no exaggeration of Richard's physical deformities in Shakespeare's descriptions. The historian gives him no better aspect than the dramatist. The 'History of King Richard the Third,' written by Master Thomas More about the year 1513, contains the following description of Richard, in comparing him with his brothers Edward and Clarence : —

"Richarde the third sonne, of whom we nowe entreate, was in witte and courage egall with either of them, in bodye and prowesse farre under them bothe, little of stature, ill fetured of limmes, croke backed, his left shoulder much higher than his right, hard favoured of visage."

Holinshed drew largely upon Sir Thomas More and Grafton for his material. Shakespeare obtained his information directly from Holinshed rather than from More or Grafton. From the second edition of Holinshed's Chronicles, published in 1586, the following description of Richard is transcribed : —

"As he was small and little of stature, so was he of bodie greatlie deformed; the one shoulder higher than the other; his face was small, but his countenance cruell, and such, that at the first aspect a man would judge it to savour and smell of malice, fraud, and deceit.

"When he stood musing, he would bite and chew busilie his nether lip; as who said that his fierce nature in his cruell bodie alwaies chafed, stirred and was ever unquiet."

So much for Shakespeare's historical accuracy in his description of Richard's physical defects.

When Shakespeare makes Richard say, —

"I am determined to prove a villain,"

and in 'Henry VI.' puts into his mouth the terrible self-imprecation, —

"Then since the heavens have shap'd my body so,
Let hell make crook'd my mind to answer it,"

then draws a picture of Richard which carries out his determination into blackest deeds
of villany and most hellish crookedness of
mind, there is justification for it all in the
historic records.

Sir Thomas More ·represents Richard's
moral nature to be as deformed as his physical : —

"He was malicious, wrathfull, envious, and
from afore his birth ever forwarde. . . . Hee was
close and secrete, a deepe dissimuler, lowlye of
counteynaunce, arrogant of heart, outwardly
coumpinable where he inwardly hated, not let-
ting to kisse whome hee thoughte to kyll : dis-
pitious and cruell, not for evill will alway, but
after for ambicion, and either for the suretie or
encrease of his estate. Frende and foo was
muche what indifferent, where his advauntage
grew, he spared no mans deathe, whose life
withstoode his purpose."

Holinshed wrote in the same strain : —

"Now when his death was knowne, few lamented, and manie rejoiced. The proud brag-
ging white bore (which was his badge) was
violentlie rased and plucked downe from everie
signe and place where it might be espied : so ill
was his life, that men wished the memorie of
him to be buried with his carren corps. He

reigned two yeers, two moneths and one daie
(too long by six and twentie months, and foure
and twentie houres in most mens opinions, to
whome his name and presence was as sweet and
delectable, as his dooings princelie and his person amiable). . . . The dagger which he ware,
he would (when he studied) with his hand plucke
up and downe in the sheath to the midst, never
drawing it fullie out : he was of a readie, preg-
nant, and quicke wit, wilie to feine, and apt to
dissemble : he had a proud mind, and an arrogant stomach, the which accompanied him even
to his death, rather choosing to suffer the same
by dint of sword, than being forsaken and left
helplesse of his unfaithfull companions, to preserve by cowardlie flight such a fraile and un-
certaine life, which by malice, sicknesse, or
condigne punishment was like shortlie to come
to confusion. Thus ended this prince his mor-
tall life with infamie and dishonor, which never
preferred fame or honestie before ambition,
tyrannie and mischiefe.''

In the above estimate of Richard's character, Holinshed has quoted freely from Grafton,
an earlier chronicler.

It is singular that Malone should have been
of the opinion that Shakespeare was not indebted to 'The Mirour for Magistrates' in
the composition of this tragedy. He says :
" The Legend of King Richard III., by

Francis Seagars, was printed in the first edition of The Mirrour for Magistrates, 1559,
and in that of 1575 and 1587; but Shakespeare does not appear to be indebted to it.
In a subsequent edition of that book printed
in 1610 the old legend was omitted, and a
new one inserted by Richard Niccols, who
has very freely copied the play before us."
A perusal of the edition of 'The Mirour for
Magistrates' published in 1587, ten years
before Shakespeare's play was published, will
reveal almost as much material for a tragedy
of 'Richard III.' as may be found in More,
Grafton, or Holinshed. It is sufficient to
quote from the table of contents to show how
fully the reign of Richard III. is therein
treated. The work contains poems under
the following titles : —

"60. How King Henry the Sixt, a vertuous
Prince, was after many other miseryes, cruelly
murdered in the Tower of London, the 22. of
May. Anno. 1471.

"61. How George Plantagenet, thyrd sonne
of the Duke of Yorke, was by his brother King
Edward wrongfully imprysoned, and by his
brother Richard miserably murdered, the 11.
of January. Anno 1478.

"64. How the Lord Hastings was betrayed
by trusting too much to his evill Councellour

Catesby, and villanously murdered in the Towre of London, by Richard Duke of Glocester, the 13. of June. Anno 1483.

" 66. The complaynt of Henry Stafford, Duke of Buckingham.

"67. How Collingbourne was cruelly executed for making a foolish rime.

" 68. How Richard Plantagenet Duke of Glocester, murdered his brothers children, usurping the Crowne : and in the 3. yeare of his raigne, was most worthely deprived of life and Kingdome in Basworth plaine, by Henry Earle of Richmond, after called King Henry the Seaventh : the 22. of August. 1485.

" 73. How Shores wife, King Edward the fourths concubine, was by King Richard despoyled of all her goods, and forced to doe open penaunce."

Here would seem to be a rich field of resources for the dramatist, as all the persons figuring in the poems mentioned above are to be found in Shakespeare's tragedy of ' Richard III.'

In these poems the same character is given to Richard that may be found in More, Grafton, Holinshead, and Shakespeare.

In the poem on Lord Rivers occur the lines : —

" The Duke of Glocester that incarnate devill
Confedred with the Duke of Buckingham,

With eke Lord Hastings, hasty both to evill
To meete the King in mourning habit came,
(A cruell Wolfe though clothed like a Lambe.) "

In the poem on 'The complaynt of Henry
Stafford, Duke of Buckingham,' that con-
spirator is made to say : —

" For having rule and riches in our hand
Who durst gaynesay the thing that wee averd?
Will was wisedome, our lust for law did stand,
In sort so straunge, that who was not afeard,
When hee the sounde but of King Richard heard?
So hatefull waxt the hearing of his name,
That you may deeme the residue of the same.

.   .   .   .

So cruell seemde this Richard third to mee,
That loe myselfe now loathde his cruelty."

The poem on ' Richard Plantagenet, Duke
of Glocester,' is prefaced with the remark of
the supposititious story-teller : —

" I have here King Richards tragedy. . . .
For the better understanding whereof, imagine
that you see him tormented with Dives in the
deepe pit of Hell, and thence howling this
which followeth.

' What heart so hard, but doth abhorre to heare
The rufull raigne of me the third Richard?' " etc.

The poem represents Richard as confess-
ing his cruelties; acknowledging that he

"right did not regard," that in him "trust turned to treason," and

" Desire of a Kingdom forgetteth all kindred."

He says : —

" For right through might I cruelly defaced."

His crimes, he admits, brought the curses of men and God upon him, —

" For which I was abhorred both of yong and olde,
But as the deede was odious in sight of God and
   man,
So shame and destruction in the end I wan."

At the close of the poem the reader of it is made to say : —

" When I had read this, we had much talke about it. For it was thought not vehement enough for so violent a man as King Richard had been."

In defending the uncertain and broken metre of the poem, the reader says : —

" It is not meete that so disorderly and un-naturall a man as King Richard was, should observe any metricall order in his talke : which notwithstanding in many places of his oration is very well kepte : it shall passe therefore even as it is though too good for so evill a person."

Thus, in all these old authors, the villanous, diabolical character of Richard is set
forth with most vigorous language.

Shakespeare seems completely justified in
painting his dramatic portrait with the darkest
colors, and on the authority of the historians
he holds, "as 't were, the mirrour up to
nature."

History justifies the bitter warning of Queen
Margaret : —

> " O Buckingham, beware of yonder dog;
> Look, when he fawns, he bites; and when he bites,
> His venom tooth will rankle to the death :
> Have not to do with him, beware of him ;
> Sin, death, and hell, have set their marks on him;
> And all their ministers attend on him."

Richard's mother, the Duchess of York, was
historically justified in heaping upon the head
of her cruel son the following accusations : —

> ". . . . . . . thou know'st it well,
> Thou cam'st on earth to make the earth my hell.
> A grievous burden was thy birth to me ;
> Tetchy and wayward was thy infancy;
> Thy school-days frightful, desperate, wild and
>   furious ;
> Thy prime of manhood, daring, bold, and venturous ;
> Thy age confirm'd, proud, subtle, sly, and bloody,
> More mild, but yet more harmful, kind in hatred :
> What comfortable hour canst thou name,
> That ever grac'd me in thy company ? "

The very conscience of Richard, as Shakespeare represents it, accords with the verdict
of history : —

" My conscience hath a thousand several tongues,
And every tongue brings in a several tale,
And every tale condemns me for a villain.
Perjury, perjury, in the high'st degree ;
Murder, stern murder, in the dir'st degree ;
All several sins, all us'd in each degree,
Throng to the bar, crying all, — Guilty ! guilty ! "

Richmond's estimate of Richard is that of
history : —

" A bloody tyrant, and a homicide ;
One rais'd in blood, and one in blood establish'd ;
One that made means to come by what he hath,
And slaughter'd those that were the means to
help him ;
A base foul stone, made precious by the foil
Of England's chair, where he is falsely set ;
One that hath ever been God's enemy."

It must appear conclusive that Shakespeare
did not depart from history in depicting the
character of Richard III., but that in the
darkest, most diabolical aspect of it he was
supported by truth and fact.

It is interesting to trace to their sources
the obscure references and seemingly far-
fetched incidents which appear quite fre-

quently in Shakespeare's lines, and have an historical basis.

In Richard's first soliloquy reference is made to a certain prophecy : —

" And, if King Edward be as true and just,
  As I am subtle, false, and treacherous,
  This day should Clarence closely be mew'd up
  About a prophecy, which says — that G
  Of Edward's heirs the murderer shall be.
  Dive, thoughts, down to my soul! here Clarence
    comes.

(*Enter* CLARENCE, *guarded, with* BRAKENBURY.)

Brother, good day : What means this armed guard,
That waits upon your grace ?
    Clar.   His majesty,
Tendering my person's safety, hath appointed
This conduct to convey me to the Tower.
    Glos. Upon what cause ?
    Clar.   Because my name is — George.
    Glos. Alack, my lord, that fault is none of yours ;
He should, for that, commit your godfathers : —
O, belike, his majesty hath some intent,
That you shall be new christen'd in the Tower.
But what 's the matter, Clarence ? may I know ?
    Clar. Yea, Richard, when I know ; for, I protest,
As yet I do not : But, as I can learn,
He hearkens after prophecies, and dreams ;
And from the cross-row plucks the letter G,
And says — a wizard told him, that by G
His issue disinherited should be ;
And, for my name of George begins with G,
It follows in his thought, that I am he.

These, as I learn, and such like toys as these,
Have mov'd his highness to commit me now."

In 'The Mirour for Magistrates' may be found these lines, put into the mouth of the Duke of Clarence : —

" For by his Queene two Princelyke sonnes he had,
Borne to be punisht for their parents synne :
Whose Fortunes balked made the father sad,
Such wofull haps were found to be therein :
Which to avouch, writ in a rotten skin
A prophesie was found, which sayd a G,
Of Edwards children should destruction bee.

" Mee to bee G, because my name was George
My brother thought, and therefore did mee hate,
But woe be to the wicked heads that forge
Such doubtfull dreames to breede unkinde debate :
For God, a Gleve, a Gibbet, Grate, or Gate,
A Gray, a Griffeth, or a Gregory,
As well as George are written with a G."

In the poem on Lord Rivers, in the same book, reference is made to this prophecy, but with a different interpretation.

" Sir Thomas Vaughan chafing cryed still :
This tyrant Glocester is the gracelesse G
That will his brothers children beastly kyll."

Holinshed mentions this prophecy in his 'Life of Edward IV. : ' —

" Some have reported, that the cause of this noble mans death rose of a foolish prophesie,

6

which was, that after K. Edward one should reigne, whose first letter of his name should be a G. Wherewith the king and queene were sore troubled, and began to conceive a greevous grudge against the duke and could not be in quiet till they had brought him to his end. And as the divell is woont· to incumber the minds of men which delite in such divelish fantasies, they said afterward, that that prophesic lost not his effect, when after king Edward, Glocester usurped his kingdome."

In the remarkable dialogue of the wooing scene between Lady Anne and Gloster, pointing to the corpse of Henry VI., Anne cries :

"O, gentlemen, see, see ! dead Henry's wounds
Open their congeal'd mouths, and bleed afresh !
Blush, blush, thou lump of foul deformity ;
For 't is thy presence that exhales this blood
From cold and empty veins, where no blood dwells ;
Thy deed, inhuman and unnatural,
Provokes this deluge most unnatural."

This incident in the drama is based not only on the superstition that it was supposed the wounds of the victim bled afresh at the approach of the murderer, but also upon this record found in Holinshed's Chronicle : —

"The dead corps on the Ascension even was conveied with billes and glaves pompouslie (if you will call that a funerall pompe) from the

Tower to the church of saint Paule, and there laid on a beire or coffen barefaced, the same in presence of the beholders did bleed; where it rested the space of one whole daie. From thence he was caried to the Black-friers, and bled there likewise : and on the next daie after, it was conveied in a boat, without priest or clerke, torch or taper, singing or saieng, unto the monasterie of Chertsie, distant from London fifteene miles, and there was it first buried."

In Act II. Scene 3, a citizen is made to cry, —

" Woe to that land that 's govern'd by a child ! "

Sir Thomas More records these words in the oration of the Duke of Buckingham in the " yeld hall in London." Buckingham is haranguing the people in the interest of Richard, and dwelling upon his merits for the high office which he seeks, —

"Which roume I warne you well is no childes office. And that the greate wise manne well perceived. When hee sayde : *Veh regno cujus rex puer est.* Woe is that Realme, that hathe a chylde to theyre Kynge."

Reference is here made to Ecclesiastes x. 16 : —

"Woe to thee, O land, when thy king is a child."

Shakespeare, however, must have found this thought in More's 'Life of Richard III.,' or in Holinshed, who has transcribed the same oration from More or Hall into his own 'Life of Edward V.'

At a council held in the Tower (Act III. Scene 4) there are present Buckingham, Stanley, Hastings, the Bishop of Ely, Catesby, Lovel, Gloster, and others. For some unknown reason Gloster sends the Bishop of Ely from the Council on a very singular errand in these words : —

" *Glos.* My lord of Ely, when I was last in Holborn,
I saw good strawberries in your garden there ;
I do beseech you send for some of them.
Ely. Marry, and will, my lord, with all my heart."

The Bishop retires, and after a short time re-enters with, —

" Where is my lord protector ? I have sent for these strawberries."

There seems to be very little, if any, sense in this strawberry incident, yet it was not invented by Shakespeare. It occurs in More and Holinshed in the following language : —

" These lordes so syting togyther comoning of thys matter, the protectour came in among them, fyrst aboute IX. of the clock, saluting

them curtesly, and excusying himself that he
had ben from them so long, saieng merely that
he had bene a slepe that day. And after a little
talking with them, he sayd unto the Bishop of
Elye : My lord, you have very good strawberies
at your gardayne in Holberne, I require you
let us have a messe of them. Gladly my lord
quod he, woulde god I had some better thing
as redy to your pleasure as that. And therwith in al the hast he sent hys servant for a
messe of strawberies."

Gloster withdraws from the Council for
about an hour and returns. As he re-enters
the Council with Buckingham the following
dialogue takes place : —

" *Glos.* I pray you all, tell me what they deserve,
That do conspire my death with devilish plots
Of damned witchcraft ; and that have prevail'd
Upon my body with their hellish charms ?
Hast. The tender love I bear your grace, my lord,
Makes me most forward in this noble presence
To doom the offenders : Whosoe'er they be,
I say, my lord, they have deserved death.
Glos. Then be your eyes the witness of their evil,
Look how I am bewitch'd ; behold mine arm
Is like a blasted sapling, wither'd up :
And this is Edward's wife, that monstrous witch,
Consorted with that harlot, strumpet Shore,
That by their witchcraft thus have marked me.
Hast. If they have done this deed, my noble lord, —
Glos. If I Thou protector of this damned strumpet,
Talk'st thou to me of ifs ? — Thou art a traitor : —

Off with his head : — now, by Saint Paul I swear,
I will not dine until I see the same. —
Lovel, and Catesby, look, that it be done ;
The rest that love me, rise, and follow me."

The original version of this incident as
given by More, and transcribed into the
Chronicles of Hall and Holinshed has been
very closely followed by Shakespeare, as will
appear by the following, taken from More's
' Life of Richard III. : ' —

" The protectour sette the lordes fast in comoning, and therupon praying them to spare hym
for a little while, departed thence. And sone
after one hower betwene X. and XI. he returned
into the chamber among them, al changed with a
wonderful soure angrye countenaunce, knitting
the browes, frowning and froting and knawing on
hys lippes, and so sat him downe, in hys place :
al the lordes much dismaied and sore merveil-
ing of this maner of sodain chaunge, and what
thing should him aile. Then when he had
sitten still a while, thus he began : What were
they worthy to have, that compasse and ymagine
the distruccion of me, being so nere of blood
unto the king and protectour of his riall person
and his realme. At this question, al the lordes
sat sore astonied, musyng much by whome thys
question should be ment, of which every man
wyst himselfe clere. Then the lord chamberlen,
as he that for the love betwene them thoughte

he might be boldest with him, aunswered and
sayd, that thei wer worthy to bee punished as
heighnous traitors whatsoever they were. And
al the other affirmed the same. . . . Then said
the protectour: ye shal al se in what wise that
sorceres and that other witch of her coun-
sel Shoris wife with their affynite, have by
their sorcery and witchcraft wasted my body.
And therwith he plucked up hys doublet sleve
to his elbow upon his left arme, where he
shewed a werish withered arme and small,
as it was never other. And therupon every
mannes mind sore misgave them, well per-
ceiving that this matter was but a quarel. . . .
Netheles the lorde Chamberlen aunswered and
sayd: certainly my lorde if they have so hei-
nously done, thei be worthy heinouse punishment. What quod the protectour thou servest
me I wene with iffes and with andes, I tel the
thei have so done, and that I will make good
on thy body traitour. And therwith as in a
great anger, he clapped his fist upon the borde
a great rappe. At which token given, one cried
treason without the chambre. . . . And anon
the protectour sayd to the lorde Hastings : I
arest the traitour. What me my Lorde quod he.
Yea the traitour, quod the protectour. . . .
Then were they al quickly bestowed in divers
chambres, except the lorde Chamberlen, whom
the protectour bade spede and shryve hym a
pace, for by saynt Poule (quod he) I wil not to
dinner til I se thy hed of."

In Act III. Scene 2, the following dialogue occurs : —

"*Hast.* Cannot thy master sleep these tedious
     nights ?
Mess. So it should seem by that I have to say.
First, he commends him to your noble lordship.
Hast. And then, —
Mess. And then he sends you word, he dreamt
To-night the boar had rased off his helm."

In the fourth scene Hastings is made to
say : —

" Woe, woe, for England ! not a whit for me ;
    For I, too fond, might have prevented this :
    Stanley did dream, the boar did rase his helm ;
    But I disdain'd it, and did scorn to fly.
    Three times to-day my foot-cloth horse did stumble,
    And startled, when he look'd upon the Tower,
    As loath to bear me to the slaughter-house."

More and Holinshed are Shakespeare's authorities for the subject matter of the above-
mentioned incidents.

More writes : —

"A marveilouse case is it to here, either the
warnings of that he shoulde have voided, or
the tokens of that he could not voide. For
the self night next before his death, the lord
Stanley sent a trustie secret messenger unto
him at midnight in al the hast, requiring hym to
rise and ryde away with hym, for he was dis-

posed utterly no longer to bide : he had so fereful
a dreme, in which him thoughte that a bore with
his tuskes so raced them both bi the heddes,
that the blood ranne aboute both their shoul-
ders. And forasmuch as the protector gave
the bore for his cognisaunce, this dreme made so
fereful an impression in his hart, that he was
thoroughly determined no longer to tary, but
had his horse redy, if the lord Hastinges wold
go with him to ride so far yet the same night,
that thei shold be out of danger ere dai . . .

" Certain it is also, that in the riding toward
the tower, the same morning in which he was be-
hedded, his horse twise or thrise stumbled with
him almost to the falling, which thing albeit
eche man wote wel daily happeneth to them to
whom no such mischaunce is toward : yet hath
it ben of an olde rite and custome, observed as a
token often times notably foregoing some great
misfortune."

Holinshed follows More word for word in
recording the above incidents.

Gloster urges Buckingham to appear before
the people to shake their confidence in the
legitimacy of Edward and Clarence (Act III.
Scene 5) : —

" *Glos.* Go, after, after, cousin Buckingham.
The mayor towards Guildhall hies him in all post : —
There, at your meetest vantage of the time,
Infer the bastardy of Edward's children :

Buck. Doubt not my lord ; I 'll play the orator,
As if the golden fee, for which I plead,
Were for myself : and so, my lord, adieu.
　　Glos. If you thrive well, bring them to Baynard's
　　castle ;
Where you shall find me well accompanied,
With reverend fathers, and well-learned bishops."

They meet again in the court of Baynard's
castle (Act III. Scene 7) : —

" *Glos.* How now, how now ? What say the citizens ?
Buck. Now by the holy mother of our Lord,
The citizens are mum, say not a word.
　　Glos. Touch'd you the bastardy of Edward's chil-
　　dren ?
　　Buck. I did ; . . .

　．　　．　　．　　．　　．　　．　　．

I bade them that did love their country's good,
Cry — *God save Richard, England's royal king !*
　　Glos. And did they so ?
　　Buck. No, so God help me, they spake not a word ;
But, like dumb statuas, or breathing stones,
Star'd on each other, and look'd deadly pale.
Which when I saw, I reprehended them ;
And ask'd the mayor, what meant this wilful silence ;
His answer was, — the people were not us'd
To be spoke to, but by the recorder.
Then he was urg'd to tell my tale again ; —
Thus saith the duke, thus hath the duke inferred ;
But nothing spoke in warrant from himself.
When he had done, some followers of mine own,
At lower end o' the hall, hurl'd up their caps,
And some ten voices cried, *God save king Richard !*
And thus I took the vantage of those few, —

Thanks, gentle citizens, and friends, quoth I ;
This general applause, and cheerful shout
Argues your wisdom, and your love to Richard :
And even here brake off, and came away."

Sir Thomas More gives in full Buckingham's oration, which was historically spoken
for the very purpose indicated by Shakespeare
in the drama. More has also left on record
the effect of the oration on the people : —

"When the duke had saied, and looked that
the people whome he hoped that the Mayor had
framed before, shoulde after this proposicion
made, have cried, king Richarde, king Richarde : all was husht and mute, and not one
word aunswered thereunto. . . . And by and by
somewhat louder, he rehersed them the same
matter againe in other order and other wordes.
. . . But were it for wonder or feare, or that
eche looked that other shoulde speake fyrste :
not one woorde was there aunswered of all the
people that stode before, but al was as styl as
the midnight, . . . when the Mayor saw thys
he wyth other pertners of that counsayle, drew
aboute the duke and sayed that the people had
not ben accustomed there to be spoken unto
but by the recorder. . . . At these wordes the
people began to whisper among themselves
secretly, that the voyce was neyther loude nor
distincke, but as it were the sounde of a swarme
of bees, tyl at the last in the nether ende of the

hal, a bushement of the dukes servants and
Nashefeldes and other longing to the protectour,
with some prentises and laddes that thrust into
the hal amonge the prese, began sodainely at
mennes backes to crye owte as lowde as their
throtes would gyve : king Richarde kinge Richarde, and threwe up their cappes in token of joye.
And they that stode before, cast back theyr
heddes mervaileling thereof, but nothing they
sayd. And when the duke and the Maier saw
thys maner, they wysely turned it to theyr purpose. And said it was a goodly cry and a joyfull
to here, every man with one voice no manne
sayeng nay."

In this matter Holinshed transcribes literally
from Sir Thomas More.

When, in Act IV. Scene 2, Richard pro-
poses to Buckingham to make way with Edward, the Duke hesitates, and asks for time
to consider the matter. This angers Richard,
who descended from his throne, gnawing his
lip and muttering : —

" *K. Rich.*   I will converse with iron-witted fools,
And unrespective boys; none are for me,
That look unto me with considerate eyes ; —
High reaching Buckingham grows circumspect. —
Boy, ——
    Page. My lord.
    K. Rich. Know'st thou not any whom corrupting
       gold
Would tempt unto a close exploit of death ?

Page. I know a discontented gentleman,
Whose humble means match not his haughty mind :
Gold were as good as twenty orators,
And will, no doubt, tempt him to anything.
K. Rich. What is his name?
Page.   His name, my lord, is Tyrrel.
K. Rich. I partly know the man ; Go, call him
hither, boy."

The page brings Tyrrel into the presence
of Richard, who engages him to make way
with

" . . . those bastards in the Tower."

This incident is based upon, but is a slight
modification of, the historical record to be
found in Holinshed and More. It appears
that Richard sent one John Grene with a
letter to Sir Robert Brakenbury, constable
of the Tower, requesting him to put the
princes to death. Brakenbury refused to
commit the murder. Grene returned with
the refusal to Richard, —

"wherwith he toke such displeasure and
thought, that the same night, he said unto a
secrete page of his : Ah whome shall a man
trust? those that I have broughte up myselfe,
those that I had went would most surely serve
me, even those fayle me, and at my commannde-
mente wyll do nothyng for me. Sir quod his
page there lyeth one on your paylet without,

that I dare well say to do your grace pleasure,
the thyng were right harde that he wold refuse,
meaning this by sir James Tyrell, which was
a man of right goodlye personage, and for
natures gyftes, woorthy to have served a muche
better prince, if he had well served god, and
by grace obtayned as muche trouthe and good
wil as he had strength and witte. . . . For upon
this pages wordes king Richard arose, and
came out into the pailet chamber, on which he
found in bed sir James and sir Thomas Tyrels,
of parson like and brethren of blood, but nothing of kin in condicion.   Then said the king
merely to them: What? sirs, be ye in bed so
soone, and calling up syr James, brake to him
secretely his mind in this mischievous matter.
In whiche he founde him nothing strange," etc.

In Act IV. Scene 4, Margaret speaks of
Richard as

" That dog, that had his teeth before his eyes,
    To worry lambs, and lap their gentle blood."

And the Duchess of York, addressing Richard, says : —

" A grievous burden was thy birth to me."

In ' Henry VI.' the King addresses Gloster
with the reproachful words : —

"Thy mother felt more than a mother's pain,
    And yet brought forth less than a mother's hope ;
        .   .   .   .

Teeth had'st thou in thy head, when thou wast born,
To signify, — thou cam'st to bite the world."

After stabbing the King, Gloster soliloquizes : —

> "Indeed, 't is true, that Henry told me of;
> For I have often heard my mother say,
> I came into the world with my legs forward;
>
> .   .   .   .
>
> The midwife wonder'd; and the women cried,
> *O, Jesus bless us, he is born with teeth !* "

More and Holinshed give the historical basis for these incidents of the birth of Richard referred to in Shakespeare's drama : —

> "It is for trouth reported, that the Duches his mother had so muche a doe in her travaile, that shee coulde not bee delivered of hym uncutte : and that hee came into the worlde with the feete forwarde, as menne bee borne outwarde, and (as the fame runneth) also not untothed."

In Act IV. Scene 4, Richard entreats Queen Elizabeth to plead his suit with her daughter.

> "*K. Rich.* Then in plain terms tell her my loving
> tale.
> *Q. Eliz.* Plain and not honest, is too harsh a style.
> *K. Rich.* Your reasons are too shallow and too
> quick.

> *Q. Eliz.* O, no, my reasons are too deep and
> dead ; —
> Too deep and dead, poor infants, in their graves.
> *K. Rich.* Harp not on that string, madam ; that is
> past.
> *Q. Eliz.* Harp on it still shall I, till heart-strings
> break."

As the figure " Harp not on that string "
occurs in More's ' Life of Richard III.,' it is
reasonable to suppose, though it had long
been a common expression, that Shakespeare
borrowed it from More or from Holinshed,
though he uses it in a different connection
and puts it into the mouth of a different
person.

The Lord Cardinal engages in a discussion
with Queen Elizabeth on the use and abuse
of sanctuary, in which Lord Howard joins.
The latter by an indiscreet remark brings a
mild rebuke upon himself. Sir Thomas More
writes : —

" The Cardinall made a countinance to the
other Lord, that he should harp no more upon
that string."

In the histories these words are spoken in
the presence of Elizabeth, but are addressed
by the Cardinal to Lord Howard ; in the
drama they are addressed to Elizabeth by

Richard. It is very probable that Shakespeare found the suggestion in the history.

On the eve of the day of battle Richard,
having made arrangements for the conflict,
proceeds to his tent with, —

"So, I am satisfied. Give me a bowl of wine:
I have not that alacrity of spirit,
Nor cheer of mind, that I was wont to have."

This corresponds with the historical record
as found in Holinshed : —

" His heart being almost damped, he prog-
nosticated before the doubtfull chance of the
battell to come; not using the alacritie and
mirth of mind and countenance as he was accustomed to doo before he came toward the
battell."

The ghost scenes and the troubled dreams
of Richard on the eve of battle, so vividly
represented by the masterly pen of Shakespeare, were not purely imaginary and created
for dramatic effect ; they were based on history or tradition, and belonged to the life and
experience of Richard.

No less than eleven ghosts rise to predict
disaster for Richard in the approaching battle ;
they are the ghosts of his murdered victims,

and their appearance fills him with terror. As they vanish he starts from his dream, with, —

"Give me another horse, — bind up my wounds, —
Have mercy, Jesu ! — Soft ; I did but dream.
O coward conscience, how dost thou afflict me !
The lights burn blue. — It is now dead midnight.
Cold fearful drops stand on my trembling flesh.
What do I fear ? Myself ? there 's none else by :
Richard loves Richard ; that is, I am I.
Is there a murderer here ? No ; — Yes ; I am :
Then fly, — What, from myself ? Great reason :
    Why ?
Lest I revenge. What ? Myself on myself ?
Alack ! I love myself. Wherefore ? for any good,
That I myself have done unto myself ?
O, no : alas, I rather hate myself,
For hateful deeds committed by myself.
I am a villain : Yet I lie, I am not.
Fool, of thyself speak well : — Fool, do not flatter.
My conscience hath a thousand several tongues,
And every tongue brings in a several tale,
And every tale condemns me for a villain.
Perjury, perjury, in the high'st degree ;
Murder, stern murder, in the dir'st degree ;
All several sins, all us'd in each degree, —
Throng to the bar, crying all, — Guilty ! guilty !
I shall despair. — There is no creature loves me ;
And, if I die, no soul will pity me ; —
Nay, wherefore should they ? since that I myself
Find in myself no pity to myself.
Methought, the souls of all that I had murder'd
Came to my tent : and every one did threat
To-morrow's vengeance on the head of Richard."

On the morning of the fatal day, Ratcliff enters Richard's tent, when the trembling King says : —

"O Ratcliff, I have dream'd a fearful dream ! —
What thinkest thou ? Will our friends prove all true ?
Rat. No doubt, my lord.
K. Rich. Ratcliff, I fear, I fear, —
Rat. Nay, good my lord, be not afraid of shadows.
K. Rich. By the apostle Paul, shadows to-night
Have struck more terror to the soul of Richard,
Than can the substance of ten thousand soldiers,
Armed in proof, and led by shallow Richmond."

The historical basis for such dramatic representation as the above may be found in the following passages from More, Grafton, and Holinshed. More says : —

"I have heard by credible report of such as wer secrete with his chamberers, that after this abbominable deede done, he never hadde quiet in his minde, hee never thought himself sure. Where he went abrode, his eyen whirled about, his body privily fenced, his hand ever on his dager, his countenance and maner like one alway ready to strike againe, he toke ill rest a nightes, lay long wakyng and musing, sore weried with care and watch, rather slumbered than slept, troubled wyth fearful dreames, sodainly somme tyme sterte up, leape out of his bed and runne about the chamber, so was his restles herte continually tossed and tumbled with the tedious impression and stormy remembrance of his abominable dede."

Holinshed moralizes on the disturbed condition of Richard's mind : —

"Than the which there can be no greater torment. For a giltie conscience inwardlie accusing and bearing witnesse against an offendor, is such a plague and punishment, as hell itself (with all the feends therein) can not affoord one of greater horror and affliction."

In Grafton's Chronicles it is written : —

"In the meane season, Kyng Richarde . . . marched to a place meete for two battayles to encounter by a Village called Bosworth, not farre from Leycester, and there he pitched hys fielde, refreshed hys souldyours and toke his rest. The fame went that he had the same night a dreadfull and a terrible dreame, for it seemed to him beyng a sleepe that he sawe dyvers ymages like terrible Devils which pulled and haled him, not suffering him to take any quiet or rest. The which straunge vision not so sodainly strake his hart with a sodaine feare, but it stuffed his head and troubled his minde with many dreadfull and busie imaginations. . . . And least that it might be suspected that he was abashed for feare of his enemies, and for that cause looked so pitteously, he recyted and declared to his familiar friends in the morning

his wonderful vision and terrible dreame. But
I think this was no dreame, but a punction and
prick of his sinnefull conscience, for the conscience is so much more charged and aggravate
as the offence is greater and more heynous in
degree."

Holinshed adds to Grafton's words his own
moralizing : —

"So that king Richard, by this reckoning,
must needs have a woonderfull troubled mind,
because the deeds that he had doone, as they
were heinous and unnaturall, so did they excite
and stirre up extraordinarie motions of trouble
and vexations in his conscience."

Now, if the Primrose Criticism would laugh
when ghosts rise before the tent of Richard,
let it laugh at Sir Thomas More, Grafton, Holinshed, tradition, and history ; not at Shakespeare, who merely dramatized the incident.

The orations of Richard and Richmond
on the field of battle Shakespeare has con-
densed from Grafton's and Holinshed's
Chronicles, where they appear in full. The
dramatist has preserved the ideas expressed,
and, in many cases, the language and figures
used by the historians. So closely do the
speeches of Richard and Richmond, as they
appear in Shakespeare, follow those found in

Holinshed, that they would be considered plagiarisms if put into the mouths of other persons.

In the historic oration Richard speaks of the "beggarly Britons" and "faynt harted Frenchmen" who come against them. In the play he calls them

> " A sort of vagabonds, rascals, and runaways,
> A scum of Bretagnes and base lackey peasants ; "

and he cries : —

> " Let 's whip these stragglers o'er the seas again ;
> Lash hence these over-weening rags of France ;
> These famished beggars weary of their lives."

In speaking of Richmond, in the historic oration, he says : —

"And to begin with the erle of Richmond, capteine of this rebellion, he is a Welsh milke-sop, a man of small courage, and of lesse experience in martiall acts and feats of warre, brought up by my moothers meanes and mine, like a captive in a close cage in the court of Franncis duke of Britagne ; and never saw armie," etc.   (Holinshed.)

In the dramatic oration Richard says : —

> " And who doth lead them, but a paltry fellow,
> Long kept in Bretagne at our mother's cost ?

> A milk-sop, one that never in his life
> Felt so much cold as overshoes in snow ? "

Richmond says, in his historic oration : —

" I doubt not but God wil rather aide us (ye and fight for us). . . . Our cause is so just that no enterprise can be of more vertue, both by the lawes divine and civile." (Grafton.)

In the play he says : —

" God, and our good cause, fight upon our side."

Again, the Chronicles put these words into Richmond's mouth : —

" What can be more honest, goodly, or godly quarrell than to fight against a Captayne, being an homicide, and a murderer of his owne blood, and progenie ?

" Who will spare yonder tirant, Richard Duke of Glocester untruly calling himself king, considering that he hath violated, and broken both the lawe of God and man, what vertue is in him, which was the confusion of his brother, and murtherer of his Nephewes ? "

In the play Richmond says : —

" For what is he they follow ? truly, gentlemen,
A bloody tyrant, and a homicide ;
One rais'd in blood, and one in blood establish'd ;
One that made means to come by what he hath,

And slaughter'd those that were the means to help
   him ;
A base foul stone, made precious by the foil
Of England's chair, where he is falsely set ;
One that hath ever been God's enemy : " etc.

This interesting comparison of the speeches
of the play with the speeches of the chronicle might be followed still further ; but enough
has been done to show that the drama does
not vary from history in the substance of these
battle harangues.

It is acknowledged that this short chapter
cannot, even as a whole, claim to be an ex-
haustive comparison of the play of 'Richard
III.' with the historical authorities on which it
is based. There are many other incidents in
the play the origin of which might easily be
traced to tradition and history ; but a sufficient
number of illustrations have been produced to
indicate beyond all question the true sources
of the subject matter of 'Richard III.'

It may be found in several instances that
Shakespeare has written nonsense, for which
critics hold him responsible, when the nonsense is the result of the historian's mistakes
or weaknesses. Historical accuracy is one of
the merits of this tragedy of 'Richard III.,'
"wherein," says Milton, "the Poet us'd not

much Licence in departing from the truth of History, which delivers him a deep Dissembler, not of his affections only, but of Religion."

The Richard of Shakespeare is the Richard of History.

PART III.

THE HISTRIONIC RICHARDS.

"Suit the action to the word, the word to the action; with this special observance, that you o'erstep not the modesty of nature: for anything so overdone is from the purpose of playing, whose end, both at the first, and now, was, and is, to hold, as 't were, the mirrour up to nature: to show virtue her own feature, scorn her own image, and the very age and body of the time, his form and pressure."

THE HISTRIONIC RICHARDS.

HE stage is not the best interpreter of Shakespeare. It has been the most efficient corrupter of that supreme dramatist. The mutilations of the original text, the interpolations and eliminations, which have rendered it almost impossible to determine what Shakespeare originally wrote, have originated in the theatre. Very few of the actors of the English stage have been scholars, though many of them have ranked with men of highest native intellectuality and taste.

Many a genius has been able to catch the spirit of Shakespeare's characters, and to present upon the stage thrilling and captivating performances, who has lacked the knowledge, learning, critical acumen, and literary taste necessary to a thorough and scientific study

of Shakespeare as a literature. It is well
known that Kemble, Cooke, Kean, and
J. B. Booth made some of their most telling
" points " by glaring misinterpretations of
Shakespeare's thought. It has not infre-
quently transpired that the actor has given to
a Shakespearian character an interpretation
which, while it stamped the performance with
the actor's genius or eccentricity, almost destroyed its Shakespearian identity. The student and scholar of to-day owe more to
Pope, Theobald, Hanmer, Johnson, Steevens,
Malone, Ulrici, Goethe, Gervinus, Collier,
Halliwell-Phillipps, and Richard Grant White,
for present light on everything that is Shakespearian in literature, than to all the actors
that have strutted the stage from the days of
Burbage to the age of Salvini, Irving, and
Edwin Booth. Actors have not enriched the
theme by any valuable restorations to the
text, any wise verbal criticism, any antiquarian research and discovery, any etymological
or grammatical elucidations, any historical or
classical illustrations of importance. For all
these important helps to the study and com-
prehension of Shakespeare we are indebted
to men of letters and of the academic gown
rather than to men of the sock and buskin.

It is nevertheless interesting to consider the merits of those great actors who by common consent have been the finest interpreters of Shakespeare on the stage. In calling to our attention the greatest Richards of the theatre it is not surprising that we are compelled to summon before us the greatest actors, the most conspicuous histrionic geniuses that have graced the English stage. No mean actor has ever been able to worthily represent Richard III., which fact must add peculiar lustre to the fame of its author.

The first, the original Richard, was a friend and a fellow actor of Shakespeare, and doubtless studied the great character in the light of its author's instruction. This was Richard Burbage, " England's great Roscius." He was born in 1566, two years after the great poet, and died in 1619, surviving his illustrious friend but three years. The name of this renowned actor appears second in the list of Principal Actors, of which Shakespeare's is first, printed in the first folio edition of the poet's works. Reference has already been made to the Tooley anecdote, in which both Burbage and Shakespeare assume the name of Richard III. The story would indicate that Burbage was as univer-

sally recognized to be the actor of the character as Shakespeare was to be the author of it.

In a play performed at one of the Uni-
versities, while Burbage was performing this
tragedy and making fame in the character of
Richard, the actor is represented as teaching
an apt pupil how to perform the part ; which
would also seem to intimate that he was
recognized to be the Richard of his day, and
the authority on the subject so far as the
theatrical representation of the character was
concerned. In the literature of his day,
Burbage is perhaps more conspicuously and
eulogistically identified with this than with any
other character which he assumed. Bishop
Corbet represents that when he visited Bosworth field his host confounded Burbage with
Richard in describing the battle, showing what
a profound impression the actor had made
in this character.

" Besides what of his knowledge he could say,
He had authentic notice from the play,
Shown chiefly by that one perspicuous thing,
That he mistook a player for a King ;
For when he should have said, here Richard died
And called 'a horse, a horse ' — he Burbadge
cried."

Burbage must have resembled Garrick in
universality and versatility of genius, as he

assumed all the most important Shakespearian characters with ability and success. In his death the theatrical, if not the literary world mourned the disappearance from the stage of all these great characters, — his " Young Hamlet, though but Scant of breath," "poor Romeo," " Tyrant Macbeth, with unwash'd bloody hand," " the red-hair'd Jew," " the grieved Moor," — and all his parts, " From ancient Leare to youthful Pericles ; " but it was above all felt by that age that in Burbage's death,

" *The* Crookback, as befits, shall cease to live."

In stature, Burbage was short and thick-set ; his features were wonderfully expressive, as the lines of the elegy run : —

" Thy stature small, but every thought and mood
Might thoroughly from thy face be understood."

His every action was truth and grace, and his voice and elocution were enchanting.

" How did his speech become him, and his pace
Suit with his speech, and every action grace
Them both alike, while not a word did fall
Without just weight to ballast it withal.
Had'st thou but spoke with Death, and us'd the power
Of thy enchanting tongue at that first hour

S

Of his assault, he had let fall his dart
And quite been charm'd with thy all-charming
   art."

If the eulogies may be accepted, Burbage
has had no superior on the stage, not even
excepting Garrick or Kean. What, then,
must have been that Richard, which was his
greatest representation, and which he undoubtedly studied and performed with Shakespeare's assistance? No reliable traditions
have come down to us of his " points " and
peculiar excellences in this character. His
creation — for he was beyond dispute the
original Richard — seems to have perished
with him. Crookback, as was fit, did cease to
live. A hundred years passed by ere another
rose to assume the almost forgotten character.
Across those years no definite, intelligent
ideas of Burbage's performance had come.
The great Burbage and the great Richard,
like the greater Shakespeare, passed away
without leaving to the historian a satisfying
portion, nor even to the curious more than a
few dry crumbs of tradition.

Thomas Betterton was doubtless in some
of his characters the equal if not the superior
of Burbage. Pepys wrote: " I only know
that Mr. Betterton is the best actor in the

world," and of this actor's first soliloquy in
'Hamlet,' he exclaimed : " It 's the best acted
part ever done by man." Yet Betterton did
not make any fame in the character of Richard. His corpulency and general ungainly
and clumsy proportions unfitted him for this
character, though his voice, not unlike Kean's
and Cooke's in natural gruffness, might have
been adapted to the part. The greatest
Hamlet, however, was not even a tolerable
Richard. Colley Cibber, who, in 1700, mutilated the play of 'Richard III.' to adapt it
to the stage, attempted the leading role, but
failed. Barton Booth, so distinguished in
Addison's ' Cato,' could not master the energy
and genius to produce

" That excellent grand tyrant of the earth."

Macklin, —

" . . . . . the Jew
That Shakespeare drew,"

was unequal to the task of performing a great
Richard.

The first actor to pick up the long-neglected
mantle of Burbage and assume with originality
and success the character of Richard III.,
was Lacy Ryan, who began to attract attention about the year 1712. This now almost

forgotten actor was doubtless the creator of
the Richard of the modern stage. To him
Garrick, Cooke, Kean, and Booth were indebted for many of their " points." Foote
was so impressed with Ryan's acting in this
part that he wrote to his praise : —

" From him succeeding Richards took the cue,
And hence his style, if not the color, drew."

Fitzgerald, the biographer of Garrick, ac-
knowledges the great actor's indebtedness
to Ryan, and Garrick himself attributed the
merits of his own representation to Ryan,
whom he had gone to ridicule in the play
of ' Richard III.,' but came away to admire,
praise, and imitate.

Ryan's Richard must have received its
excellences from his mental rather than from
his physical advantages. If so, the greater
the virtue and more just the praise. While
Ryan's general features were favorable, his
nose had been broken by a blow, and his
cheeks pierced and jaw broken by a bullet.
The result of these injuries was an irremedi-
able defect of voice and elocution. He gave
but little attention to his " make up," and
often appeared in a part with slovenly dress,
which, with a lack of natural grace and his

absolute ignorance of gesture, detracted from
the external merits of his representation. In
spite of these disadvantages, however, he made
an impression in the character of Richard III.,
which has come down, through the imitations
of the greatest actors, to the present time.
Lacy Ryan must have possessed an uncommon genius to have risen above all his physical defects into a character which is in
many important features the stage Richard
of to-day.

On Oct. 19, 1741, David Garrick made his
debut at Goodman's Fields as Richard III.
It was a wise choice of character, though one
of the most trying parts that ever actor attempted. His debut was not only a success,
but his performance of Richard was the sensation of the day. All London was in a furor
of dramatic excitement ; and the *élite* of the
city thought it no task to drive out to Goodman's Fields to witness the great Shakespearian representation, while even the most
distinguished congratulated themselves on their
good fortune if they succeeded in reaching the
door and crowding into the packed and over-
flowing theatre. Men and women of fashion
and of letters talked of nothing else but the
great Garrick and his wonderful Richard. The

actor at once rose to the distinction of merit-
ing and receiving the criticism of Walpole,
the praise of Pope, and the social attentions
of Chesterfield. It was in the character of
Richard III. that Garrick first achieved celebrity, and in this character he increased to the
end the unfading laurels of his histrionic fame.
The morning after his debut in ' Richard III.'
his reception was acknowledged by the press
to have been "the most extraordinary and
great that was ever known on such an occasion." Macklin declared that this was one
of the characters in which "the little fellow"
secured his own immortality. Mrs. Elizabeth
Montague wrote at the time : —

"On Saturday, I intend to go to Goodman's
Fields to see Garrick act Richard the Third,
that I may get one cold from a regard to sense,
I have sacrificed enough to folly, in catching
colds at the great puppet-shows in town."

When Pope went to hear Garrick he carried
with him a strong prejudice for Betterton's
style, which was dignified but stagy, mouth-
ing, and declamatory, while Garrick's style
was most natural both in action and in elocution. Pope was captured at once, and, to
the intense satisfaction of the actor, applauded

with the applauding house. Garrick seems
to have been as deeply moved that night by
the presence and approbation of Pope as
Pope was by the acting of Garrick, for the
actor says : —

" When I was told that Pope was in the house,
I instantly felt a palpitation at my heart, a tu-
multuous, not a disagreeable emotion in my
mind. I was then in the prime of youth, and
in the zenith of my theatrical ambition. It gave
me a peculiar pleasure that *Richard* was my
character when Pope was to see me and hear
me. As I opened my part I saw our little
poetical hero dressed in black, seated in a
side box near the stage, and viewing me with
a serious and earnest attention. His look shot
and thrilled like lightning through my frame,
and I had some hesitation in proceeding from
anxiety and from joy. As *Richard* gradually
blazed forth the house was in a roar of applause,
and the conspiring hand of Pope shadowed me
with laurels."

To know what impression Garrick made
on Pope, listen to his euthusiastic eulogy : —

" That young man never had his equal as an
actor, and he will never have a rival."

When Garrick acted this part to Peg Wof-
fington's Lady Anne in Dublin, in 1742, the

town went mad, and so powerful was Garrick's acting that "women shrieked at Richard's death."

Garrick had a handsome face, capable of marvellous expression, full of animation and intelligence. His general physical proportions were neither great nor inferior, but were all grace and nobleness. His voice was full, rich, and commanding, and capable of expressing every emotion of the heart. In style he was himself alone, and hence the founder of a new school of acting. He was natural, versatile, and intellectual. No quality of an actor seemed wanting in him, with the possible exception of stature. He was qualified in body and mind, in genius and art, to give the theatrical world such a Richard as it had not looked upon since the famous days of Burbage. Walpole pronounced it " as perfect as could be."

Dr. Doran has given us as fine and perhaps as accurate a description of Garrick in the part of Richard as may be found : —

" From the moment the new actor appeared they saw a Richard and not an actor of that personage. Of the audience he seemed unconscious, so thoroughly did he identify himself with the character. He surrendered himself

to all its requirements, was ready for every
phase of passion, every change of humor, and
was as wonderful in quiet sarcasm as he was
terrific in the hurricane of the battle scenes.
Above all, his audiences were delighted with
his 'nature.' Since Betterton's death, actors
had fallen into a rhythmical, mechanical, sing-
song cadence. Garrick spoke not as an orator,
but as King Richard himself might have spoken.
The chuckling exultation of "So much for
Buckingham!" was long a tradition on the
stage. His 'points' occurred in rapid succession. The rage and rapidity with which he
delivered

    ' Cold friends to me! What do they in the North,
      When they should serve their sovereign in the
        West?'

made a wonderful impression on the audience.
Hogarth has shown us how he *looked*, when
starting from his dream; and critics tell us that
his cry of 'Give me another horse!' was the
cry of a gallant man; but that it fell into one
of distress as he said, 'Bind up my wounds,'
while the 'Have mercy, Heaven,' was moaned
on bended knee. The battle scene and death
excited the enthusiasm of an audience altogether
unused to acting like this."

Other "points" by which he would electrify
an audience were, his hurling away the Prayer
Book after he had, with the bishops, closed

his conference with the mayor and citizens;
his wild, terrified start from sleep in the tent;
the desperation with which he fought in the
battle scene; the terrible exhibition of will
and determination in the death scene, where
his hands would convulsively clutch the sod
and his fingers dig into the very earth. The
impetuosity, suddenness, and terrific energy of
action at every climax of tragic interest made
the entire performance one of the most remarkable in the history of the stage.

The impression which Garrick made upon
the tragic nature of Mrs. Siddons in his performance of Richard has been recorded in the
'Life of John Taylor,' and is valuable in proportion as Mrs. Siddons was a judge of great
tragedy. Taylor says : —

"Speaking of Garrick, once when the subject
of acting was introduced in company with Mrs.
Siddons, I observed so long a time had passed
since she saw him act, that perhaps she had
forgotten him; on which she said emphatically,
it was impossible to forget him. Another time
I told her that Mr. Sheridan had declared Garrick's Richard to be very fine, but did not think
it terrible enough. 'God bless me!' said she,
'what could be more terrible?' She then in-
formed me, that when she was rehearsing the part
of *Lady Anne* to his *Richard*, he desired her,

as he drew near her from the couch, to follow
him step by step, for otherwise he should be
obliged to turn his face from the audience, and
he acted much with his features. Mrs. Siddons
promised to attend to his desire, but assured
me there was such an expression in his acting
that it entirely overcame her, and she was
obliged to pause, when he gave her such a look
of reprehension as she never could recollect
without terror."

If he owed much to Ryan for the merits of
his Richard, it is Garrick's glory that all subsequent representations have been considered
great in proportion as they have approximated
the marvellous excellences of his performance.
During Garrick's supremacy several actors
entered the field to rival him even in the
character of Richard. Aaron Hill in 1744
wrote to his friend Mallet that he had heard
Garrick in Macbeth and was highly pleased :

"He is natural, impressed, and easy; has a
voice articulate, and placid: his gesture never
turbulent, and often well adapted; is untouched
by affectation. His peculiar talent lies in pen-
sively preparatory attitudes; whereby, awakening expectation in the audience, he secures
and holds fast their attention. . . . I intend
to see him quite through *Richard*, — where
I have been told, he is thought strongest. I

design to see, too, Mr. *Quin*, who has, they say,
gone new and noble lengths, in the same character. And, when I have observed them both,
you shall have my opinion, very frankly."

Thus Quin was considered a rival of Garrick ; but, though he was the Falstaff of his
day, his "new and noble lengths" in the
character of Richard never brought him into
decent comparison with Garrick.

Two very respectable Richards appeared,
however, in the performances of Thomas Sheridan and Henry Mossop. Richard III. was
Sheridan's first and Mossop's second character. When Sheridan made his debut in Dublin as Richard, he was as much of a sensation
in the Irish capital as Garrick had been in
the English metropolis. He was young and
handsome, gifted with a natural grace, a
mellow voice, and a fine intellect. He had
the genius and ability successfully to rival
Garrick in King John, which actually created
jealousy in the bosom of the monarch of the
stage. Mossop was an actor of intelligence
and college training ; he had a finely pro-
portioned body of medium stature, and a
voice of great compass, full, rich, and melodious, well adapted to tragedy. He rivalled
Garrick in Othello, as Sheridan did in King

John, but he could not win very bright laurels
in Richard in competition with the "little
fellow." Mossop and Sheridan were rivals,
and public sentiment was about evenly di-
vided on the question as to which should
stand second only to Garrick in the character
of Richard. Mossop's performance is remembered more for its eccentricities than its real
merits. His elocution was almost ludicrously
deliberate, his gestures were very awkward,
and his dress, singular to relate, was white
satin puckered!

After Garrick, the next truly great Richard
to appear, was that erratic genius, George
Frederick Cooke, who made his debut at
Covent Garden Theatre, Oct. 31, 1800, in
the tragedy of 'Richard III.' His performance immediately established his reputation
as an actor of the first rank. The stage had
seen no Richard to compare with Cooke's
since the brilliant days of Garrick, and even
the memory of that great actor's powers did
not cast a shadow over Cooke's splendid
representation. Cooke had the advantage of
having seen Garrick in this his most celebrated character; and it held him in good
stead, for there can be no doubt that he
followed Garrick in certain "points." His

acting in Richard produced a sensation. He wrote of the reception which he received : —

"Never was a reception so flattering. Never did I receive more encouraging, indulgent and warm approbation than that night, both through the play and at the conclusion."

His first play in America was 'Richard III.,' in which he appeared at the Park Theatre, New York, Nov. 21, 1810. It was considered the greatest performance that had ever been seen on the American stage. Richard was Cooke's most celebrated character; he became identified with it in the public mind as Betterton did with Hamlet, Macklin with Shylock, Henderson with Falstaff, Barry with Othello, Kemble with Coriolanus, and Macready with Virginius. As Doran said of Garrick, so may it be said of Cooke, he was Richard, not a mere actor of that personage. In his interesting "Reminiscences," Henry Crabb Robinson in speaking of Cooke says :

"We were so lucky as to see him in *Richard,* his favorite character. Nature has assisted him greatly in the performance of this part, his features being strongly marked and his voice harsh. I felt at the time that he personated the ferocious tyrant better than Kemble could have done."

Leigh Hunt declared that Cooke was for some time the greatest performer of Richard. This opinion was held for a time by Macready, who said, " He was the Richard of his day." And further, Macready says : —

" My remembrance of George Frederick Cooke, whose peculiarities added much to the effect of his performance, served to detract from my confidence in assuming the crooked back tyrant. Cooke's varieties of tone seemed limited to a loud harsh croak descending to the lowest audible murmur ; but there was such significance in each inflection, look, and ges- ture, and such impressive earnestness in his whole bearing, that he compelled your attention and interest."

Again, in speaking of this same performance, Macready says : —

" Cooke's representation of the part I have been present at several times, and it lived in my memory in all its sturdy vigor. I use this expression as applicable to him in the character which Cibber's clever stagy compilation has given to an English audience as ' Richard Plan- tagenet,' in place of Shakespeare's creation — the earnest, active, versatile spirit, ' *impiger*, *iracundus*, *inexorabilis*, *acer*,' who makes a business of his ambition, without let or demur clearing away or cutting down the obstacles to

his progress, with not one pause of compunc-
tious hesitation. There was a solidity of de-
portment and manner, and at the same time a
sort of unctuous enjoyment of his successful
craft, in the soliloquizing stage villainy of
Cooke, which gave powerful and rich effect to
the sneers and overbearing retorts of Cibber's
hero, and certain points (as the peculiar mode
of delivering a passage is technically phrased)
traditional from Garrick were made with consummate skill, significance and power."

Leslie pronounced Cooke " the best *Richard* since Garrick ; " and C. M. Young
" considered him without a rival " in that
character. John Howard Payne gives us his
impressions of this great actor as he first appeared on the American stage in the tragedy
of ' Richard III. : ' —

" As regards Cooke, I was at the first performance of Cooke in America. He made a
different impression upon me from any other
actor I have ever seen ; there was something
so exclusively unique and original in his dramatic genius. He always presented himself to
me in the light of a discoverer, one with whom
it seemed that every action and every look
emanated entirely from himself; one who appeared never to have had a model, and who
depended entirely upon himself for everything
he did in the character he represented. Cooke

reminds me of no one but himself, and I have never been able to recognize the real *Richard* in any other actor than Cooke."

This opinion has great force when it is known that Payne was intimate with Kean, whom many considered to be the greatest Richard that had ever lived, not even excepting Garrick.

Cooke was, as Robinson intimates, remarkably well adapted to this character by nature. He possessed a manly figure of medium stature, a noble and intellectual face, with a high broad forehead, a prominent nose, an expressive mouth, a strong chin, and splendid, dark, fiery eyes. His features, however, wore a naturally proud, sarcastic, and even sneering expression. His arms were very short, and were used with little regard to the rules of graceful gesture ; yet this very natural defect, added to the awkwardness of his gait and motion, made his performance of the crooked-back Richard all the more impressive. He had two voices : one was bitter, harsh, croaking ; and the other mild, smooth, and persuasive. In his playing of Richard he would make rapid transitions from one voice to the other with singular and startling effect. Leigh Hunt gives us one of the se-

9

crets of Cooke's power in Richard when he
says : —

" Mr. Cooke is, in fact, master of every species
of hypocrisy.   He is great in the most impu-
dent hypocrisy, such as that of Sir Pertinax
MacSycophant and of Richard III."

It was this natural sarcasm, this haughty,
cynical disposition, that enabled Cooke to
play the first three acts of ' Richard III.' with
a power peculiar to himself.   Though he took
his cue from Garrick, he did not seem, like
that great actor, to have made his most telling
points in the tent scene and in the battle
scene.   It was in those scenes which called
for cunning, hypocrisy, and villany, that he excelled, — not in the scenes of greatest energy
of action, but in those where words and looks
are most significant.   According to Dunlap,
Cooke's " superiority over all other Richards "
was acknowledged to be " in the dissimula-
tion, the crafty hypocrisy, and the bitter sarcasm of the character."   It has been claimed,
however, that his craftiness and villany were
too apparent.   Instead of hiding his cunning
and hypocrisy he advertised it in every look
and gesture, and every intonation of his voice.
His acting was considered strong but coarse,

forcible but almost too brutal. And yet his representation in the opinion of play-goers must
have been original, thrilling, superb. When
he stepped before the footlights of old Park
Theatre for the first time, he was fifty-four
years old, and his constitution was badly
shattered by intemperance ; yet, says Dunlap
his biographer, "his appearance was pictu-
resque and proudly noble, his head elevated,
his step firm, his eye beaming fire." Cooke
was as great in the wooing scene with Lady
Anne as Garrick was in the tent scene. All
the arts and powers of sarcasm, "wheedling
flattery," hypocritical humility, cunning suavity,
velvet-tongued villany, were brought into play ;
and such a piece of consummate acting had
rarely if ever before been seen. One of the
most sensational " points " in the acting of
Cooke and Garrick was made with this line
which Shakespeare did not write, but which
Cibber interpolated into his " adaptation," —

" Off with his head — so much for Buckingham."

Cooke was original and sensational, if not
correct, in pronouncing these words very de-
liberately, as he stood swaying backward and
forward. Other actors, including Garrick,
have spoken them in hot haste, and have

characterized this whole part of the messenger
scene with rapidity and impetuosity of feeling
rather than with Cooke's cool, sardonic delib-
eration. No actor has represented in the
character of Richard greater villany and con-
temptible hypocrisy with less kingliness and
heroism than Cooke. In Garrick's performance one of the most striking features was,
not the diabolical plotting and planning of
murders, the cunning, oily-tongued flattery
and insinuation, but rather the courageous,
desperate, almost heroic fight and death on
Bosworth field. Cooke could not leave this
same impression ; his mean, cunning, devilish murderer of women and children, his
sneering, flattering, hypocritical Richard, could
not fight gloriously. He who was so incom-
parably mean, detestable, fawning, dog-like, in
the presence of Lady Anne could not be gallant and manly in the presence of Richmond.
Cooke could not act the heroic. He had not
the heroic element in his own nature. And
it is significantly true that not a single noble-
souled, large-hearted, generous man has been
able to bring to the stage a great representation of Richard, if exception be made of Burbage, whose personal character is too slightly
known to be criticised. It may be claimed

that Garrick was an exception; but it will be
found that Garrick was one of the most envious,
self-conceited, and mean-souled actors of his
day, though in his histrionic supremacy he
could have afforded to be most generous and
great-hearted. Cooke was proud, overbearing,
insolent, cynical, drunken, and misanthropic,
possessed of a genius which might have found
expression in deeds of personal villany had it
not found an outlet, a vent, upon the stage in
the character of Richard III.

John Philip Kemble was the founder of a
school which emphasized the dignified, ornate,
scholarly, and graceful in acting, — a school
to which have belonged such artists, if not geniuses, as J. P. Kemble, Charles Kemble, C.
M. Young, W. C. Macready, Thomas Cooper,
Lawrence Barrett, and Henry Irving.

Kemble and Cooke were contemporaries
and jealous rivals. Their methods, however,
were dissimilar; and as a consequence, there
were characters in which each excelled the
other. Kemble's Coriolanus, Hamlet, and
Macbeth were superior to Cooke's; but
his Richard, like his Sir Giles Overreach,
"came not within a hundred miles of Cooke."
Kemble would not act Richard after he had
seen Cooke's performance. There were, how-

ever, excellences in Kemble's representation
that would have made it popular had it not
been for the greater representation of his
rival.

Kemble was a solid, dignified, and graceful
actor, who sought to produce a great whole,
an evenly balanced and harmonious representation. He did not attempt by sudden and
unexpected bursts of passion to gain applause.
He would not sacrifice the symmetry and
dramatic proportions of a play to a few startling and original " points." If he did not
possess Cooke's genius, he was admired for
a sober judgment, a refined taste, a nobility
of mind, and a general culture and art of
manner and method which were not found
in Cooke. Kemble was a man of splendid
physical proportions, his bearing was manly
and dignified, his features were handsome
and noble, every movement of his body was
grace ; but he lacked voice and spirit. Though
every representation of his was marked by sin-
cerity, taste, and careful study, yet it was often
cold, hard, and unimpassioned. Hence he
who was superb in Coriolanus could make
no very profound impression in Richard III.
That character, however, received at his hands
an interpretation which was very satisfactory

to some critics. Kemble preceded Cooke in
this character, and was embarrassed by the
memory of Garrick, as he was the first, with
the unimportant exception of Henderson, to
suffer comparison with him. Kemble's representation possessed the merit of originality.
Cooke took his cue from Garrick ; had he
attempted an original representation he might
have created less of a sensation. The physical beauty and noble proportions of Kemble
were out of harmony with the deformity of
Richard, and as Sir Walter Scott remarks,
" from the noble effect of his countenance
and figure, neither could he seem constitu-
tionally villanous ; he could never *look* the
part of Richard, and it seemed a jest to hear
him, whose countenance and person were so
eminently fine, descant on his own deformity."
Kemble was not endowed with that bitter,
misanthropic, sneering disposition, which held
Cooke and Kean in good stead in the character of Richard. He lacked also the energy,
which he sacrificed to grace, to fill the whole
stage with the desperate, vehement, terrible
action of the usurper. He could not, or
would not, rise to the climaxes of " dreadful
energy " which characterized Garrick's performance, nor work up to the " frightful pas-

sion " of a Junius Brutus Booth. He lacked
force, intensity, and action.

There were, notwithstanding these faults,
certain marked and valuable characteristics
in Kemble's representation which will forever
preserve it from inferiority, if they do not
elevate it above mediocrity. While in the
acting of Garrick, Cooke, Kean, and Booth,
the villany of Richard was apparent in every
gesture, look, and intonation, in Kemble's
artistic representation it was covered up
by a semblance of virtue and nobility.
Kemble's Richard did not advertise his diabolism on all his features, nor proclaim it in
all his vocal inflections. This dignified actor
used to argue, as Scott says, "that Richard
III., being of high descent and breeding,
ought not to be vulgar in his appearance, or
coarse in his cruelty." And Scott intimates
that Kemble incorrectly gave to Richard not
only "a tinge of aristocracy," but represented
him to be "of a generous and chivalrous
character " and a " handsome prince." This
representation was relieved of the uninterrupted darkness and terror of Cooke's and
Garrick's performances. There came in upon
those horrible scenes occasional rays of light
through Kemble's interpretation, which not a

few welcomed, not only as original, but as correct and artistic. It is singular, however, that two critics of ability can study a performance of this character and disagree as to what merits it lacks or possesses. Charles Lamb admired certain features of Kemble's Richard, and lamented that "the sportive relief which he threw into the darker shades of Richard disappeared with him." Lamb saw the "sportive relief" of Kemble's performance. Henry Crabb Robinson says, in speaking of Cooke's performance: "I felt at the time that he personated the ferocious tyrant better than Kemble could have done. There is besides a sort of humor in his acting which appeared very appropriate, and which I think Kemble could not have given." Robinson saw "a sort of humor" in Cooke's Richard, but could not, like Lamb, see it in Kemble's. In the wooing of Lady Anne, Kemble was weak, as he was in the closing scenes of the tragedy; that is to say, his faults were in scenes which demand great hypocrisy and villany, and in scenes of impetuosity and rush of action. He excelled in the soliloquies of the play, and in scenes where there is a demand for dignity and princely bearing.

As Cooke and Kemble were waning, there flashed upon the English stage the light of a new and incomparable genius, — Edmund Kean. It is doubtful whether a greater Richard was ever seen. No traditions of Burbage or Garrick· were able to cast his wonderful performance into shade. It was perhaps the most original, and in all its parts the most wonderful, representation that had appeared since the days of Burbage and Shakespeare.

Cooke followed Garrick, and some have charged that Kean imitated Cooke. This last charge is without foundation ; for greatly as Kean admired the genius of Cooke, he once told John Howard Payne that he had never seen that actor in the character of Richard. Kean's performance seems to have combined the excellences of both Garrick and Cooke. Kean and Cooke were very similar in natural disposition, in moral make-up. They were both haughty, cynical, egotistic, coarse, intemperate, and uncontrollably passionate and misanthropic. They were similarly endowed with power to represent cunning, villany, hypocrisy, and brutal cruelty. Neither of these actors had a fine, melodious voice to be compared with a Gar-

rick's or a Young's. Yet their voices did
not lack power, but possessed the quality,
which may be used with great effect in
Richard, of transition from the harsh, croaking, and bitter to the smooth, mellow, and in-
sinuating tones. Kean's physical qualifications
were inferior in many respects to Cooke's,
and also to Kemble's and Garrick's. He was
insignificant in stature; he shuffled in his
gait. He had not Cooke's expanse of brow,
strength of chin, and general nobility of
feature. Yet he had a wonderful eye, full,
black, and intense; and though his features
were not cast in a noble mould, they possessed marvellous powers of expression, so
that no actor could *look* Richard more perfectly than Kean. To this power to *look*
Richard Kean added the power to *act* him;
herein he surpassed Kemble. Though he
was fitted for the part in natural temperament, Kean possessed less natural acrimony
and meanness than Cooke, and may have
fallen behind that actor in those scenes
where this spirit is expressed; yet he had
a more impetuous, nervous, magnetic nature,
which enabled him to excel Cooke in energy
and terrific force of action, and in power
to electrify an audience by sudden and mag-

nificent outbursts of passion.   Cooke's genius
was more limited in its range than Kean's.
While the former is remembered more for
his Richard than for any other Shakespearian
character he assumed, Kean is remembered
for his greatness in Shylock and Othello as
well as in Richard.   The general verdict
seems to accord to Kean the superiority even
in Richard.   Cooke, no doubt, was incomparable in certain scenes; but, taking the
whole tragedy into consideration, Kean's was
the greater Richard.   Cooke was not known
in his character of Richard before his forty-
fifth year, when he made his debut at Covent
Garden ; but Kean's performance in this character may be traced back to his boyhood.   He
was a life-long actor of the part.   We are
indebted to C. M. Young for one of our first
glimpses of Kean's Richard.   The boy, with
his mother, Nance Carey, was strolling about
the country giving exhibitions of his histrionic
precocity, when one day about the Christmas
time he chanced to bring up at the door of
Thomas Young's hospitable mansion, and was
admitted to the hall, where Charles Young
first saw him.   Evidently the elder Young
had planned a little entertainment for the boy
and friends who had come to enjoy one of

his delightful dinners, and at the proper time
the genial host " ordered the butler to bring
in ' the boy.' "

" On his entry he was taken by the hand,
patted on the head, and requested to favor the
company with a specimen of his histrionic ability. With a self-possession marvellous in one
so young he stood forth, knitted his brow,
hunched up one shoulder-blade, and, with sardonic grin and husky voice, spouted forth
Gloster's opening soliloquy in Richard III.
He then recited selections from some of our
minor British poets, both grave and gay; danced
a hornpipe; sang songs, both comic and pa-
thetic; and, for fully an hour, displayed such
versatility, as to elicit vociferous applause from
his auditory, and substantial evidence of its sin-
cerity by a shower of crown pieces and shillings
— a napkin having been opened and spread
upon the floor for their reception. The accu-
mulated treasures having been poured into the
gaping pockets of the lad's trousers, with a smile
of gratified vanity and grateful acknowledgment,
he withdrew, . . . and left the house rejoicing.
The door was no sooner closed than every one
present desired to know the name of the youthful
prodigy who had so astonished them. The host
replied, that this was not the first time he had
had him to amuse his friends; that he knew
nothing of the lad's history or antecedents; but
that his name was Edmund Kean."

Dr. Young spoke a good word for the wonderful boy whenever opportunity offered, and recommended him to Mrs. Clarke, who finally met him with the kindly question, "Are you the little boy who can act so well?" Edmund having answered with a polite bow, the good lady further asked, "What can you act?" Without hesitation he answered, "Richard the Third, Speed the Plough, Hamlet, and Harlequin." "I should like to see you act," said the lady in admiration. "I," replied he with flushed cheeks, "should be proud to act to you." Arrangements were made for an appearance. The boy in the character of Richard astonished his auditors. All were enthusiastic in his praise, and Mrs. Clarke took him under her care to educate him for the stage.

Kean had done his rehearsing or practising in the character of Richard in a garret over a London bookstore. At the early age of fourteen he was on the stage. When engaged at Drury Lane Theatre in children's parts, he attracted the attention of notable actors and actresses by his spontaneous outbursts of tragic declamation in the green-room. On one occasion Mrs. Charles Kemble asked who was creating the disturbance, when some

one replied : " It is little Carey [Kean] re-
citing '.Richard III.' after the manner of Garrick ; go and see him, he is really very clever."
When, later in his career, Kean acted this
part in the provincial towns of Ireland and
England, he met with little success. Though
in his representation there was rising the
greatest Richard of the modern stage, the
play-goers could not appreciate it, and while
they were delighted with his ballads and jigs
they nodded over his wonderful performance
of 'Richard III.' He was hissed on one
occasion because he forgot the audience in
his complete absorption in the part ; and for
their ignorant boorish manners, Kean stepped
to the front of the stage and shouted, " Unmannered dogs ! Stand ye, when I com-
mand ! " It awed the " unmannered dogs "
to silence.

When Kean appeared at Drury Lane in
1814, at the age of thirty-one, the manager
requested him to make his debut in ' Richard
III. ; ' but the actor was too sensitive about
his physical inferiority, and shrank from appearing in a part which would place him at a
disadvantage on account of his slight stature.
He therefore insisted upon appearing as Shylock, in which he achieved unquestioned suc-

cess. With the encouragement of this triumph he ventured to appear in the character of Richard. He had almost if not quite wrested the sceptre from Macklin as Shylock; in 'Richard III.' he had to contend against the splendid traditions of Garrick and Cooke. He succeeded at least in sharing, if not in fully capturing, their laurels. His Richard at Drury Lane in 1815 was as great a hit as Garrick's at Goodman's Fields in 1741. As it was with that famous actor, so was it with Kean, "the town became his own."

Pope eulogized Garrick, and Byron went wild over Kean. The prophecy of Beverley, the Cheltenham manager, was fulfilled in about two years after it was generously uttered. Oxberry tells us that when the loafers who hissed Kean's Richard from the Cheltenham stage blamed Beverley for "suffering such a creature to do Richard," the wary manager replied : "That creature in a few years will be the greatest creature in the metropolis, and you will go far and near to get a glimpse of him." On the night of Feb. 12, 1815, Edmund Kean as 'Richard III.' was "the greatest creature in the metropolis;" nay, the greatest creature in the histrionic world. That first performance has been well described

by H. B. Baker, in his interesting work on
" Our Old Actors : " —

" He approached thé part with fear and trembling. ' I am so frightened,' he said before the
curtain rose, ' that my acting will be almost dumb
show to-night.' But nevertheless, from the first
soliloquy to the appalling last scene, he took both
audience and critics by storm. The performance
must have been wonderfully like Garrick's. . . .
Mrs. Garrick, who went to see him play it, told
Dibdin that Cooke put her in mind of her hus-
band, but Kean was like Garrick himself."

Dr. Doran has given us a striking sketch
of Kean's triumph on that memorable
occasion : —

" A few nights before he played the part, it
was performed at Covent Garden, by John
Kemble ; and a short time after Kean had
triumphed it was personated by Young; but
Kemble could not prevent, nor Young impede,
the triumph of the new actor, who now made
Richard his own, as he had previously done
with Shylock.

" His Richard (on the 12th of February) settled his position with the critics ; and the criticism to which he was subjected was, for the
most part, admirably and impartially written.
He is sometimes spoken of as ' this young
man ; ' at others, ' this young gentleman.'

10

'Even Cooke's performance,' says one, 'was left at an immeasurable distance.' A second adds, 'it was the most perfect performance of any that has been witnessed since the days of Garrick.' Of the grand effects followed by a storm of applause, a third writes that 'electricity itself was never more instantaneous in its operation.' "

Lord Byron was more enthusiastic over Kean's performance than Pope over Garrick's. He went to his room and wrote in his diary : —

"Just returned from seeing Kean in Richard. By Jove, he is a soul! Life, nature, truth, without exaggeration or diminution. Kemblé's *Hamlet* is perfect, but *Hamlet* is not Nature. *Richard* is a man; and Kean is *Richard.*"

Kean's "points" in this representation were numerous. Oxberry's criticism furnishes us with one of them : —

"In his opening soliloquy of Richard, which has been pronounced to be unequalled, he commits a glaring error, by pausing after the words 'And my first step shall be,' — as if Richard had not previously determined that it should be, — 'on Henry's head.' "

This "point" was made with one of Cibber's interpolations.

In the wooing scene with Lady Anne, his
acting was considered most original and artistic, though his hypocrisy and scorn have been
criticised as too apparent and too coarse.
Henry Crabb Robinson has given us his impressions of Kean's great performance : —

"He played *Richard*, I believe, better than
any man I ever saw ; yet my expectations were
pitched too high, and I had not the pleasure I
expected. The expression of malignant joy is
the one in which he surpasses all men I have
ever seen. And his most flagrant defect is want
of dignity. His face is finely expressive, though
his mouth is not handsome, and he projects his
lower lip ungracefully ; yet it is finely suited to
Richard. He gratified my eye more than my
ear. . . . His declamation is very unpleasant, but
my ear may in time be reconciled to it, as the
palate is to new cheese and tea. It often reminds me of Blanchard's. His speech is not
fluent, and his words and syllables are too distinctly separated. His finest scene was with
Lady Anne, and his mode of lifting up her veil
to watch her countenance was exquisite. The
concluding scene was unequal to my expectation, though the fencing was elegant, and his
sudden death fall was shockingly real."

Kean made a fine "point" out of the
lines, —

"He did corrupt frail nature with a bribe,
    To shrink my arm up like a wither'd shrub."

He would look for some time with contempt
at the puny arm, and then slap it in anger and
mortification out of his sight. It will be noticed that the lines with which Kean made
this fine and startling point do not belong to
Shakespeare's play of 'Richard III.,' but are
Colley Cibber's interpolation from 'Henry
VI.' We are again indebted to Doran for a
fine enumeration of Kean's "points" in this
representation : —

"Joyous and sarcastic in the opening soliloquy; devilish, as he passed his bright sword
through the still breathing body of Lancaster;
audaciously hypocritical, and almost too exult-
ing, in the wooing of Lady Anne ; cruelly kind
to the young Princes, his eye smiling while his
foot seemed restless to crush the two spiders
that so vexed his heart ; — in representing all this
there was an originality and a nature which were
entirely new to the delighted audience. Then
they seemed to behold altogether a new man revealed to them, in the first words uttered by him
from the throne, — 'Stand all apart !' from which
period to the last struggle with Richmond, there
was an uninterrupted succession of beauties ;
even in the by-play he found means to extort
applause, and a graceful attitude, an almost
silent chuckle, a significant glance, — even so

common-place a phrase as 'good night, my lords,' uttered before the battle of the morrow, were responded to by acclamations such as are awarded to none but the great masters of the art."

Macready was particularly impressed with Kean's wooing of Lady Anne, his interview with Buckingham when he proposed the murder of the two young Princes, and with the terrible energy with which he hurried every plan to execution. While he admired Cooke in certain parts more than Kean, he gave to the latter higher praise for his representation as a whole. It was Macready's opinion that Kean never displayed more masterly elocution than in the third act of 'Richard III.'

Hazlitt was an enthusiastic admirer of Kean in the character of Richard, declaring that "we cannot imagine any character represented with greater distinctness and precision, more perfectly *articulated* in every part." This able critic notes, among others, the following "points : " —

"He is more refined than Cooke, more bold, varied, and original than Kemble in the same character. . . . The courtship scene with Lady Anne is an admirable exhibition of smooth and

smiling villainy. . . . Mr. Kean's attitude in lean-
ing against the side of the stage before he comes
forward to address Lady Anne, is one of the
most graceful and striking ever witnessed on
the stage. It would do for Titian to paint. . . .
His by-play is excellent. His manner of bid-
ding his friends ' Good night,' after pausing with
the point of his sword, drawn slowly backward
and forward on the ground, as if considering the
plan of the battle next day, is a particularly happy
and natural thought. He gives to the two last
acts of the play the greatest animation and effect.
He fills every part of the stage. . . . The concluding scene in which he is killed by Richmond
is the most brilliant of the whole. He fights
at last like one drunk with wounds ; and the
attitude in which he stands with his hands
stretched out, after his sword is wrested from
him, has a preternatural and terrific grandeur,
as if his will could not be disarmed, and the very
phantoms of his despair had power to kill."

Sir Walter Scott gives us a glimpse of one
of Kean's "points" in acting when he refers
to "the drunken and dizzy fury with which
Richard, as personated by Kean, continues to
make the motion of striking after he has lost
his weapon."

To refer again to the ever-enjoyable Doran,
we find this picture of the closing scene, made
the more interesting by anecdote : —

"The triumph was cumulative, and it was crowned by the tent scene, the battle, and the death. Probably no actor ever even approached Kean in the two last incidents. He fenced with consummate grace and skill, and fought with an energy that seemed a fierce reality. Rae had sneered at the 'little man,' but Rae now felt bound to be civil to the great tragedian, and referring to the passage of arms in 'Richard III.,' he, having to play Richmond, asked, 'Where shall I hit you, sir, to-night?' 'Where you can, sir,' answered Kean; and he kept Richmond off, in that famous struggle, till Rae's sword-arm was weary with making passes. His attempt to 'collar' Richmond when his own sword had fallen from him was so doubtful in taste that he subsequently abandoned it; but in the faint, yet deadly-meant passes, which he made with his swordless arm, after he had received his death-blow, there was the conception of a great artist; and there died with him a malignity which mortal man had never before so terribly portrayed."

One feature of this last scene, of great force and interest, Talfourd refers to in his criticism : —

"His last look at *Richmond* as he stands is fearful; as if the agony of death gave him power to menace his conqueror with the ghostly terrors of the world into which the murderous tyrant is entering."

Kean made his first appearance in America on the 8th of January, 1821 ; he made his debut in ' Richard III.,' as Cooke had done about ten years previously. The Philadelphia theatre was crowded to excess, and he was received with the most' rapturous applause, as was the case with Cooke at the New York theatre in 1810. It is doubtful whether Kean succeeded in wresting the sceptre from Cooke, who had made a wonderful fame in America. The ' Democratic Press ' voiced the universal verdict as to the greatness of Kean in the last scene of ' Richard III. : ' —

"So much had been said of the dying scenes of Mr. Kean, that curiosity was at its *topmost round* when the fight began, *which was to issue* in his death. All that we had heard, — all that we could ever hear, on this head, must necessarily fall infinitely short of the extraordinary powers displayed by Mr. Kean in the last scene. He writhed with bodily pain ; *he agonized* under the terrors of conscience ; he *gasped* for breath ; his every motion evinced distress, and approaching death, *his* sufferings were so painful to the beholder, that *he* felt relieved when nature was exhausted and *Richard* had expired."

One or two very good anecdotes are related of Kean in connection with his cele-

brated and incomparable representation of
Richard III., showing that the admiration of
some was not founded on an independent
judgment or study of his characterization, and
also showing that all persons did not look
upon him as the greatest Richard. On the
authority of F. Reynolds, a rising and self-
conscious barrister on one occasion, in company with quite a number of political and
literary notables, took occasion to compliment Kean by saying —

"that he had never seen acting until the preceding evening. 'Indeed!' said Kean; 'why
you must have seen others, sir, I should conceive, in *Richard III.*' 'I have seen,' replied
the barrister, 'both Cooke and Kemble; but
they must excuse me, Mr. Kean, if I should
turn from them, and frankly say to you, with
Hamlet, "Here 's metal more attractive."'
Kean felt highly flattered. The conversation
then turning on a curious lawsuit, Kean, after
a pause, asked the barrister if he had ever visited the Exeter Theatre. 'Very rarely indeed,'
was the reply, 'though, by the by, now I recollect, during the last assizes, I dropped in towards the conclusion of Richard III. *Richmond*
was in the hands of a very promising young
fellow; but such a *Richard!*—such a harsh,
croaking, barn brawler! I forget his name, but'
—'I 'll tell it you,' interrupted the Drury Lane

hero, rising and tapping the great lawyer on the
shoulder: 'I'll tell it you — *Kean.*'"

'Blackwood's Magazine' is responsible for
the following story: —

"During one of Charles Kean's visits to the
United States, he was entertained at dinner by
one of the great New York merchants. Oppo-
site to him at the table there sat a gentleman,
who continued to observe him with marked at
tention, and at last called on the host to present
him to Mr. Kean. The introduction was duly
made, and ratified by drinking wine together;
when the stranger, with much impressiveness
of manner, said, 'I saw you in Richard last
night:' Kean, feeling, not unnaturally, that a
compliment was approaching, smiled blandly
and bowed. 'Yes, sir,' continued the other, in
a slow, almost judicial tone, 'I have seen your
father in Richard; and I saw the late Mr.
Cooke' — another pause, in which Charles
Kean's triumph was gradually mounting higher
and higher. 'Yes, sir; Cooke, sir, was better
than your father; and your father, sir, a long
way better than you!'"

Fanny Kemble, rising above the prejudices
of her own education, could with womanly
generosity and intelligence write: —

"Kean is gone, and with him are gone Othello,
Shylock, and Richard. . . . Who that ever saw

will ever forget the fascination of his dying eyes in *Richard*, when deprived of his sword; the wondrous power of his look seemed yet to avert the uplifted arm of Richmond. If he was irregular and unartisticlike in his performance, so is *Niagara* compared with the waterworks of Versailles."

It is said that an hour before his death Kean sprang from his couch crying, as Richard, —

" A horse, a horse, my kingdom for a horse ! "

Charles Kean, though " the son of his father," was not a chip of the old block. He attempted to follow in the footsteps of Edmund Kean, and doubtless made his great mistake in choosing those parts in which he would necessarily be compared unfavorably with that great genius. He made his American debut in ' Richard III.,' but was not able to create the enthusiasm which attended his father's performance. There seemed to be a prophecy in the words of Edmund Kean when, after acting Richard one night and looking upon a little performance of Charles at home, he said : " The name of Kean shall die with *me*. It shall be buried in my coffin." And it was.

The stage has not seen a great Richard since Kean's day ; that is to say, an original, powerful representation, to be compared with Garrick, Cooke, or Kean.

This difficult part has been attempted by nearly every Shakespearian actor, but rarely with pronounced success. Young, Cooper, Phelps, Macready, Forest, and J. B. Booth in the earlier days, and Irving, Lawrence Barrett, Wilson Barrett, and Edwin Booth in recent times, have been the great histrionic interpreters of Shakespeare in England and America. While any one of these may have had, or may have the talent to give a clever and acceptable performance of ' Richard III.,' it is doubtful whether any one of them has had the genius to create a new, original, and great Richard.

Cooper had his admirers, who claimed that Kean alone surpassed him in this character. Young attempted to eclipse Kean's performance, but signally failed, though in certain characters, on account of his physical advantages, he was Kean's superior.

Macready's talent was superior to his genius, yet he must rank with the first of actors. The stage has seldom if ever known a greater Virginius. He performed every part which he undertook intelligently and with scholarly good taste ; but he could never rise to the

heights of a Garrick, a Cooke, or a Kean in
such trying and difficult characters as Othello,
Shylock, Lear, and Richard III. Admirers
of Macready have claimed that he " determined his position as a first-class actor " by
his performance of Richard III. He had
seen Kean in this character and greatly admired him, placing him above Cooke. One
of Macready's merits was his individuality,
independence, and originality. His faults
were his own, as were his merits ; he aped
no other actor. His style was a medium between Kemble and Kean. He did not possess
all the excellences of both, but he avoided
many of their faults. He was neither as cold
as Kemble nor as fervent and magnetic as
Kean ; yet he had much of the Kemble dignity and scholarly taste, with some measure of
the spirit of Kean. His Richard therefore
was a representation that must be classed between the too princely Richard of the one
and the too villanous Richard of the other.

There was some rivalry between Macready
and Kean in this very part, and the critics
were not slow to see merits in the new actor
which the old favorite did not possess. Leigh
Hunt's comparison of these two representations is undoubtedly just, while it gives us a

fair estimate of Macready in the character
of Richard : —

" Mr. Kean's Richard is the more sombre, perhaps the deeper part of him — Mr. Macready's
the livelier and more animal part, a very con-
siderable one nevertheless. Mr. Kean's is the
more gloomy and reflective villain, rendered
so by the united effects of his deformity and
subtle-mindedness ; Mr. Macready's is the more
ardent and bold-faced one, borne up by a temperament naturally high and sanguine, though
pulled down by mortification. The one has
more of the seriousness of conscious evil in it,
the other of the gaiety of meditated success.
Mr. Kean's has gone deeper even than the
relief of his conscience, he has found melan-
choly at the bottom of that necessity for relief ;
Mr. Macready's is more sustained in his
troubled waters by constitutional vigor and
buoyancy. In short, Mr. Kean's Richard is
more like King Richard darkened by the shadow
of his approaching success, and announcing by
the depth of his desperation when it shall be
disputed ; Mr. Macready's Richard is more like
the Duke of Glocester, brother to the gay tyrant
Edward the Fourth, and partaking as much of
his character as the contradictions of the family
handsomeness in his person would allow. If
these two features in the character of Richard
could be united by an actor, the performance
would be a perfect one."

Indeed, what a performance that would be, with an actor possessing all the merits and none of the faults of Kean and Macready! But the name of Macready never calls up by association the name of Richard ; on the other hand, " Kean " and " Cooke " are almost synonymous with " Richard."

There are not a few who look upon Junius Brutus Booth as the last, but not the least, of the great Richards of the English stage. Booth's fame is almost entirely American. He was not able to sustain himself in competition with Kean in England. He made his debut at Covent Garden, London, in the character of Richard, and also made his first appearance in America in the same character. It is quite excusable in Mr. Edwin Booth that he should think his gifted father had more than half gained the victory over Kean in Richard and Lear, and carelessly threw it away as a trifle. It may be honor enough for Booth that he was a greater Hamlet than Kean or Cooke ; it adds nothing to his fame to vainly compare him with either of these geniuses in ' Richard III.' Nothwithstanding this, Richard was one of Booth's favorite and most popular parts, especially in America. This was generally his first-night character.

In London, Richmond, New York, Boston,
Philadelphia, and Pittsburgh, he first appeared
in ' Richard III.' Booth was a follower of
Kean, if not a very close and slavish imi-
tator. He may have had genius, but it was
a genius without great originality or power of
invention. He did not strike out a new line,
as did Garrick, Kemble, Kean, and Macready.
He was not unlike Kean in temperament. He
was an energetic, magnetic, impulsive actor,
quite as erratic as Cooke or Kean. He had
the natural, physical qualifications for the
character of Richard, and in certain parts
acted with great power. Booth made his
" points " in scenes requiring the greatest
action. He was greatest where Kean and
Garrick were greatest, and, even in these
scenes, reminded his hearers of the geniuses
he imitated more than he impressed them
with the originality and high order of his own
genius. He was not great in the first scenes,
where Cooke and Kemble were at their best.
There was a magnetism in his voice, a fire in
his eye, a significance in his gesture which
enabled him at times to get the better of his
hearers' judgment, and in spite of tricks and
misinterpretations, to carry them away with
enthusiasm. Certain critics declared that

"his whisper could chill the blood;" "his glance extort obedience;" "his very gesture drew tears." There can be no doubt that Booth was great in the tent scene and battle scene of 'Richard III.' Traditions and the critics seem to agree in pronouncing the fight one of the most terrific and thrilling representations ever witnessed on the stage. The picture may not be overdrawn which Stone gives us in his 'Theatrical Reminiscences :'

"The dying scene of Booth was truly frightful — his eyes, naturally large and piercing, appeared to have greatly increased in size, and fairly gleamed with fire; large drops of perspiration oozed from his forehead, and coursing down his cheeks, mingling with and moistening the ringlets of the wig he usually wore in Richard, caused them to adhere to his face, rendering his appearance doubly horrible. The remark· able portrayal of the passions, — the despair, hate, grief, — in the passage in the original text which reads —

> ' But the vast renown thou
> Hast acquired in conquering
> Richard, doth give him more,
> Than the soul departing from the body,'

has probably never been surpassed even by George Frederick Cooke, whose Richard is said to have excelled all others."

Mr. Stone would encounter some diffi-
culties in attempting to find the lines quoted
above in the original text of Shakespeare's
'Richard III.' But from this bit of remi-
niscence we learn that Booth, like the other
great Richards, made some of his most powerful and celebrated "points" with the Colley
Cibber interpolations. Ludlow has given as
accurate a description of Booth's representation, as a whole, as may perhaps be found
among reminiscences : —

"When the proper scene opened, Mr. Booth
walked on the stage, made no recognition of the
reception applause, and, in an apparently medi-
tative mood began the soliloquy of 'Now is the
winter of our discontent,' which he delivered
with seeming indifference, and with little if any
point, something after the manner of a school-
boy repeating a lesson of which he had learned
the words, but was heedless of their meaning,
and then made his exit, without receiving any
additional applause. I was not where I could
ascertain the impression made upon the audience, but on the stage, at the side scenes, the
actors were looking at each other in all kinds
of ways, expressive of astonishment and dis-
gust. I was standing near Mr. Benton, an old
actor, the *King Henry* of the evening, — and
as I turned to go away, he said, 'What do
you think of him, Mr. Ludlow?' 'Think,' I

replied, 'why, I think as I thought before, that he is an impostor! What do *you* think of him?' 'Why, sir,' said Benton, 'if the remainder of his *Richard* shall prove like the beginning, I have never yet, I suppose, seen the character played, for it is unlike any I ever saw; it may be very good, but I don't fancy it!' . . . I retained my first impression of Mr. Booth until he came to the fourth act, where, in a scene with *Buckingham*, he hints at the murder of the young princes. Then I thought I discovered something worthy of a great actor. From that on, his acting was unique and wonderful. I had never seen any one produce such effects, and come so near my ideas of the character, — not even Mr. Cooke, who was as far below Mr. Booth in the last two acts as he was above him in the first three."

This seems a very fair description and a just comparison. But it does not contradict the claim that Booth was below Cooke in the first three acts, and below Kean in the last two. Cooke was the greatest Richard in the first three acts; Kean the greatest Richard in the last two. Booth was not the greatest Richard in any act, though he may have the fame of standing next to Kean in the parts where Kean was, and is, and doubtless ever will be, first.

The Primrose Criticism merits our thanks for having prompted the fresh investigation, which has strengthened our confidence in the Shakespearian authorship of ' Richard III.' A tragedy so faithful to history, so clearly the climax of a series of plays of common origin, so unified and intensified in one great and terrible character, so universally indorsed as Shakespearian by the poets, critics, antiquarians, and Shakespearian editors of the past three hundred years, so popular with the greatest histrionic geniuses of the English stage, and so worthy of their highest efforts and most glorious triumphs, — such a tragedy is not unworthy of him who

" . . . was not of an age, but for all time."